Firefighter
The Fallen Angel

by
Gareth McCready

authorHOUSE®

AuthorHouse™ UK Ltd.
500 Avebury Boulevard
Central Milton Keynes, MK9 2BE
www.authorhouse.co.uk
Phone: 08001974150

First published by AuthorHouse 10/31/2008

ISBN: 978-1-4389-2003-0 (sc)

Printed in the United States of America
Bloomington, Indiana

This book is printed on acid-free paper.

This book is dedicated to the countless New York firefighters and 911 service men and women who bravely lay down their lives for their unknown brothers and sisters on the tragic morning of September the 11th 2001...

First of all I would like to thank my lovely wife Leanne McCready; I think she deserves a medal for putting up with me through the long days and even longer nights as I battled continuously to complete this book. I thank her for all her support over the eighteen months of hard graft. Leanne supported me from concept to completion and for that I give her first spot on the acknowledgments, thanks Leanne, you're the best. I must also thank Evelyn and David McCready for their continuous support in everything I've ever done in my life including this project; they are by far the best parents I could ever ask for, thanks for all your support guys. I know of a man who answered my call for help no matter how bizarre it seemed at the time, I know if it wasn't for this man I probably wouldn't have completed the book to such a high standard. He was first to review it, first to correct it and also the first to give me the push to complete it. It doesn't stop there for this man; some might call Justin Dougherty a computer wizard or P.C. genius. I call him a true friend, here's to you Justin, for your amazing graphical work on the front cover and countless hours of vital help through the past eighteen months, I couldn't have done it without you Justin. Another great person I would like to thank for all her hard work and professionalism is Mrs Gillian Hay. Gillian's roll in the project was vital.

As she agreed to do the first thorough proof read on the manuscript which was extremely important, Gillian did an amazing job in restructuring my work from an original screenplay format into a novel format and also correcting a lot of my spelling mistakes along the way which I must admit there were quite a few, thanks again Gillian. I must admit I enjoy reading but I enjoy it even more when the author adds in a surprising graphic from time to time. Nearing the end of my writing I thought of how a few sketches of the characters would work well through out the book, not many, just a few. It was then I asked a true champion if he would get involved in the project, knowing his passion for art and his adorning love for creation I just knew that Kieron McKinney would accept, Kieron being the shy modest fellow he is was reluctant to show me some of his finished pieces, I don't know, maybe he thought that they were not what I was looking for, however when he finally showed me his work I was gob smacked. Kieron had captured the characters the way I had envisioned them for so long, I thank you for bringing my work to life Kieron you are not only a good friend but an amazing person.

I remember when I was completing my book that the next step was to get an agent, knowing that getting an agent was probably the hardest things to get in the business I started worrying. It was this worrying that affected my writing near the end as I began to have this overwhelming feeling of self doubt. This lasted for a few weeks, I knew I had to do something so I made a decision, I sent off my unfinished manuscript to a number of literary agents hoping for good news. Each day that passed when I didn't receive a letter I became more doubtful of my work until I received a phone call from Darin Jewell of the Inspira group literary agency. Darin asked me if I would like him to represent my work, I was over the moon with joy; I couldn't believe that Darin wanted me on board. Darin, I thank you for you swift replies and the confidence you gave me through the past few months, your advice and professionalism has been fantastic, you are a true gentleman and I'm looking forward to working with you and the Inspira group in the future. Last but not least I would like to thank my entire network of friends and extended family for being there for me through out my life, your support and confidence means a lot to me, thanks again to everyone...

1

It is a brisk mid September morning in the small suburban residential area. The sound of bike wheels and kids laughing gives the close knitted community a real impression of tranquillity and peace, interrupted only by a handsome firefighter opening his creaky un-oiled front door. As he lifts the morning paper, he takes a deep breath and stands proudly as he looks upon his city from a distance.

"So, what have you got in store for me today then?" Mason whispers to himself. Looking into the clear blue sky he notices the last minutes of a faint moon light high above the city buildings. Mason glares up for a few minutes and thinks to himself,

'Now isn't that something?' He enjoys the moment for a mere second until a sharp yell from the kitchen pulls his attention away from the beautiful scene above him.

"Breakfasts on the table Mason," sounds a very rushed firefighter's wife. Finally finishing the preparations for her husband Mason, and her adorable eight year old Son Tyler, Amanda finally gets seated.

As the young family sit down together and tuck into the delicious blueberry pancakes Amanda has made, by now covered with lots of syrup and sauces, Father and Son begin talking and laughing with each other. As Amanda looks on with a smile, her proud expression is closely followed with one of sadness, creating a tear, and without warning she runs to the sink in a swift but graceful dash. As she breaks down into tears an uneasy silence falls at the table creating a tension in the air.

"Hey little buddy why don't you go to your room and get your things ready for school," Mason suggests to Tyler.

"Sure Dad," Tyler replies before making his way to the stairs remembering to take a few pancakes with him as he goes.

With Tyler out of site Mason slowly makes his way towards his wife.

"Are you ok Honey?" Mason asks while keeping his distance, knowing she will need a little space right now he stands in front of the refrigerator feeling a little frustrated.

The main problem is that Amanda has always wanted Mason to get a safer job as she couldn't bear the loss of another member of her family. This stress, coupled with amongst other things, the passing of their young daughter Lydia only two years ago means friction is not uncommon between them.

Mason plucks up the courage to comfort his wife,

"Look honey, I'm going to take the little man to school, just try to relax for a while before work." Mason says to his wife as he notices her teary eyes.

"Ok Mason, you're right, I should really pull myself together, huh!" At that moment Tyler comes running down the stairs with his school bag.

"Is my lunch ready Mom?" He asks.

"Sure it is Tyler, just let me just get it for you," sniffles Amanda. Mason kneels down to Tyler and tries explaining to him why his Mom is in this state, though he doesn't really know how to find the words. Mason hates situations like this one; but thankfully Amanda arrives back with Tyler's lunch pack releasing Mason from this tricky situation.

"I'm leaving now my two handsome men!" Amanda calls. She always makes sure that they never part on bad feelings, so she used to always use the two handsome men line, or something along those lines, for two reasons. First of all to warm Mason's heart and secondly to embarrass little Tyler, as whatever their reaction she manages to receive a kiss from each of them before she leaves. As Mason walks Amanda to the door, he turns to Tyler and whispers,

"Just a minute buddy, I'll be right back; I just have to speak to your Mom for a second." Mason throws him a wink before leaving the room.

"Sure Dad, don't be long though," Tyler jokes.

Nearing the car Mason sweeps his arms around his wife caressing her dearly, as he looks into her eyes he strongly whispers,

"Hey honey, come on, we'll get through this, you know we will, be strong honey."

"It's hard Mason, it's just so hard, every were I look I see her little face. I just keep thinking I should have been there, I should have known, but now it's too late!" As these words pass Amanda's lips Mason knows all too well of the pain she speaks of, and can do nothing but watch as she starts the car and makes her way to the local diner were she works leaving Mason with a feeling of helplessness.

Tyler's' school is en-route to the fire station. It's about a fifteen minute drive to the school. Tyler always enjoys this journey with his Dad as feels like a grown up when he rides up front in the red pickup. Mason always tells Tyler great stories of the 'Blue Angels' and of all the exciting adventures that they would experience whilst on duty. The 'Blue Angels' was the stumbled upon nick name adopted by Mason's crew a few years ago for reasons Mason keeps hidden from most people.

Tyler loves these stories of the 'Blue Angels' and he often dreams of the day when he himself will be a firefighter. All he wants in the world is to follow in his fathers footsteps.

Soon to arrive at the school, Mason tries explaining to Tyler that he and his team are to be moved to a more modern station up town and that the old one will be left empty, thankfully protected by the cities trust. The fire departments higher administration felt that the old station's historical value would guarantee it being made a listed building and therefore be cared for by the cities trust.

Tyler's eyes widened with shock, he can't believe that the Blue Angels would be leaving the station. Tyler loves the old station; he had been there many times.

It was a beautiful building in its day, with a red brick face and massive oak slat double doors for the fire engines to come and go. The building itself appeared to be built at an angle, and certain peculiarity surrounded it. Almost hidden from the main avenue, it was as if the architect was experimenting with his own creative genius. The interior of the building was also a little strange, with off angled stairs leading to somewhat hidden rooms. It was safe to say that the building was indefinably unique; so you can imagine when Mason and his crew learned of the move they passionately felt they would be leaving a part of themselves behind too.

As Tyler gets out of the pickup Mason calls to him,

"Hey, you forgot your mitt." Tyler's most prized possession in the whole world was the baseball and mitt that his old man had got for him on his seventh birthday. Tyler always carried it with him and loved it when the two of them would spend hours playing catch together out back to pass long evenings.

Mason reaches over for the mitt and steps out of the pickup meeting his Son half way.

"Come on kid, you would forget your head if it wasn't screwed on," laughs Mason whilst patting him on the head.

"Hey Dad, when can I come to work with you, I mean a real day not just for a while?" Tyler asks whilst hooking his mitt onto his blue jeans. Mason looks down at his brave little son.

"When ever you're big and strong little man, but not until then." Mason answers with a glare of ambition in his eyes. As Tyler makes his way towards the school gate, Mason remains at the front of the pickup until Tyler is out of site.

"That's my boy…" Mason whispers under his breath.

2

Across town, a run down apartment block stands facing the old docking bay. Once a bright spot full of life and home to some back street amusers willing to lend a hand for a quick buck now paints a much darker picture. The once lit cobbled docks are now run by high ranking mobsters, with crooked goons taking their slice of pie, if you will, of the illegal cargo that's being injected into the city like an incurable disease. However a struggling family needed somewhere to live leaving them no other option. Although these apartments are terrible, it does keep them from the elements.

It must have been thirty years since any maintenance was ever carried out, as the only way up is by a winding crooked stair case because the elevators had packed up a long time ago. The place was a dump! With grimy walls and loose tiles on the floor, it's safe to say that a demolition ball was long over due.

The family includes a mother *(Caroline Woods)* and her most recent partner *(Bill Grey)*, who together tries relentlessly to keep the family from falling apart. When Caroline's husband left her, Rachel and Michael *(her children)* were very young, so through the hard years she stayed strong for them, working her fingers to the bone to ensure they had a warm bed at night and food when they woke.

The makeshift parents try their up most to hold on to any dead end jobs that come their way. Bill works part-time on the docks struggling to make ends meat. Due to the organized corruption with imports and exports the high paid jobs are crooked and therefore given to the goons of Scapatechi. Scapatechi is the infamous organiser of all this corruption which makes working life just that little bit harder for an honest man.

Caroline, a maid in a dingy motel hates her job, especially as her pushy manager makes sleazy passes then humiliates her in front of other workers when he doesn't get his filthy way. However this wouldn't always be the case, as Caroline knew deep down in her heart that when it comes down to it she always does what she has to do, to survive.

Most days, an elderly neighbour by the name of Mrs Garbonee would take care of Rachel. She unfortunately for Caroline was unable to take care of both children, as she was too old to cope with the sheer energy of two little tearaways, causing Michael to be left alone without full-time supervision or guidance.

Michael spends most of his time hanging around the docks hassling goons or snooping around the old warehouses. Once one of the goons asked Michael to do a little job, nothing much, just collect a package. Unknown to Michael the package was nothing more than a few sandwiches for the goons to munch on during their morning break, however Michael thought he was involved in a major operation and ran with the package as fast as his legs would carry him, knowing that they'd throw him a quarter or two on his return. He held that package tight to his chest, not stopping until he got back to the docks. Finally returning to the docks he found himself gasping for air, when one of the goons eyeballed him and sharply snapped.

"Well pass it over kid!" The demanding goon held out his grubby finger cut gloved hand, for Michael to quickly pass over the now slightly squashed package.

"You did good kid!" The grubby goon echoed to Michael, then without warning he flipped him a quarter, it was at that moment Michael felt a part of something, he felt belonged.

Through time Bill began noticing that Michael's relationship with a few of the goons was progressing.

He knew it was wrong, he knew it was dangerous, but also knew there was nothing he could do about it. As time passed Bill became bitter about the fact his step son was involving himself with the scum that had corrupted these streets for so long, also bitter at the fact that he was loosing all respect for his family and treating his sister Rachel like garbage. Michael's actions caused nothing but burden on all their shoulders. These actions often led to Bill coming home stressed. When drunk, he would beat Michael, mostly when they were alone at home. Years of this relentless abuse caused by the vicious circle that the family became locked in affected Michael, as reflected by a steady build up of anger and sheer rage at Bills actions. This resulted in him performing many acts of arson and vandalism in the local dockland area, pushing him even closer beneath the wing of the Dragon.

Rachel, the pure soul that she was over looked her brother's bizarre behaviour until a few weeks ago when she was playing in her room with the few toys she had, Michael entered the room with a mischievous look in his eyes. "Hey Michael," a very polite angle like Rachel said. However there was no response from her brother, all he wanted to do was take her happiness away, doing so by sweeping the toys out from under her.

"Oh what a lovely doll this is!" Michael mocked sarcastically.

"Please Michael... Give her back... Please!" Rachel's voice now quivered with fear. Her sorrow was soon followed by a burst of adrenaline, which caused her to make a quick grasp for her doll. She held tightly to half while Michael held the other half. The two estranged siblings continued to fight it out, however the strain was too great for the little doll, at that moment the doll tore in two. The quick jolt of force sent Rachel back towards the wall, causing her head to hit off the red bricks with a thud. With her vision blurred and her lip shaking, she could just about make out the image of her evil brother laughing before throwing the other half of her doll to the ground.

After a few moments a very frightened and confused Rachel pulled herself to her feet, lifted her destroyed doll and slowly walked over to the window squeezing it together on the way. As she sat on the old wooden window sill she gazed across to the ray of lights, the supposed *city of dreams* that everyone often talked about which seemed a million miles away from her city of nightmares.

3

Mason pulls up at the station knowing it's going to be his last shift in the place he parks his pickup in the usual spot and slowly gets out with his eyes fixed on this beautiful building which he has known all to well. Standing back just for a few seconds admiring his so called second home, he notices the flag flying proudly in the brisk morning wind.

"Gets me every time," mutters a very honourable firefighter.

Most of the crew are already there and going about their usual duties. There is an element of sadness flowing through the air, understandable due to the circumstances; however most of the guy's spirits are still high as they talk and reminisce about their memories of working at this unique station for so long.

Mason enters and receives a warm welcome. He has gained popularity and the men's unfaltering support as he has led them through unimaginable life and death fire fights in the past. Together they made it out, together they survived the fires, and together they'd move on, as somewhat brothers rather than colleagues. As Mason begins his daily routine he can't help but think on his family; his broken wife, his passionate boy, and not forgetting his lost daughter.

Passing the workshop Mason notices a guy fixing a leak in some old pipes. "No need for that now Mr!" Mason shouts over to a somewhat startled Dale. Dale turns to Mason and gives him a smile,

"Pass me that wrench Mason, some body's going to have to look after this old place!" Dale mutters under his breath with a hint of sarcasm. With his oil stained overalls and his thick black rimmed glasses, no-one would have believed that Dale was once a great firefighter. Though due to an unfortunate heroic past he now spends his time maintaining the station. As he is no longer on active duty, Dale is kept on by the department for maintenance and odd jobs mainly because of his technical mind and hands on approach.

Dale has no close family and everyone knew that the crew was the only family he ever had, so keeping him on the payroll just seemed like the right thing to do; well, after all, the poor guy did experience a bad accident involving an eight story office block and ferocious flames, which kind of gives him the right to hang about the station, he nearly died for it!

"Well, are you all set for the big move then?" Dale asks with a raised brow. As the words leave his mouth he limps over to the workshop bench to await Mason's response.

"It's like this Dale, the longer you stay somewhere, the more you start becoming that place, we are men, we'll soon adapt to our new surroundings." Mason laughs though deep down he knew what Dale meant.

Due to his accident Dale now knows that a firefighter's job is extremely dangerous and that their safety is never fully guaranteed, therefore he spends a great deal of his spare time working on safer equipment, prototypes for the guy's to use during call-outs. However, the equipment was never officially recognised or passed by the Fire Departments higher administrators, leaving Dale no choice but to store the prototypes at the back of the workshop or boxed away in the shadows gathering dust. The inventing of these amazing creations became more of a pass time or hobby for Dale than anything else.

"What the hell is that?" Shriek's a very intrigued Mason. Mason's eyes have been caught by, and are latched on a firefighter's helmet, though no ordinary helmet.

"My God Dale, It's incredible!" Mason states, refining his voice. The helmet was completely reshaped, more streamline, more durable with a blacked out visor to protect the eyes, the helmet held a retro vintage yellow colour through which Mason could see distinctive dark scuff marks which added to its unique and distinctive look.

"Oh you like that, do you?" A smug Dale sharply asks.

"Can you keep a secret?" Mason didn't answer Dale, he just gave him a look as much to say, should you even have to ask!

"Take a look at this!" Dale whispers, whilst looking up and down the corridor in a suspicious manor. Mason follows a limping Dale to the rear of the workshop towards an empty locker bay; not knowing what the heck Dale has been working on, Mason's imagination starts to run wild until they finally reach their destination.

Out of sight from most people, there it hung in the shadows like an old friend. It is a huge dusty three quarter length fire jacket. The jacket has the faded colours of the department and scorch marks were Dale has been testing its resistance. Dale explains to Mason that the durability of the jacket is perfect, completely fire resistant and very fashionable he adds, though Mason knew that part was from Dale's strange sense of humour.

The interior of the jacket is fitted with a harness, containing all kinds of instruments and gadgets.

"My God Dale, some of this stuff is amazing; we really ought to get some of these prototypes recognised!" Mason states with heart. For years Dale had tried to get the equipment passed, however due to the departments financial setup they just didn't see the logic in spending more money than they felt was needed.

At the station the atmosphere has now become a little more relaxed and begins to feel like a retirement party. With all the crew sitting in the main lounge area relaxing, exchanging stories and playing cards; basically guys just being guys. When they hear the alarm bell, none of them wanted to believe it was real. They thought they would be spending their last shift at the station. Better yet, they thought they would spend it actually *in* the station; Typical. However they are professionals with a job to do and have a purpose, so within seconds the team is on the move. The call is a fire reported in the old apartment blocks down in dockland.

4

"Over here!" A voice from the shadows shouts. It is the voice of Scapatechi. A charismatic character, sharply dressed with a red carination fastened to the lapel of his black pin stripped suit jacket. He is the mobs so called leading man, the wannabe godfather of New York's underworld. Organised crime, gun running, prostitution and beatings, you name it; if it's against the law he's already involved. Next, he plans to introduce a new evil for this era... Drugs! Tonight Scapatechi meets with his primary rival, Carlos Francez. Francez is pretty much as evil, but Scapatechi wants him out of the picture; he wants this new drug empire for himself. He wants it all - money, guns, drugs, POWER! The meeting with Carlos Francez could be a milestone for the city's underground crime gangs. A chance to take total control of the city's deepest, darkest, habits.

Francez stands proud with his stocky body and extremely large gut, he looks more like a world pie eating champion than an up and coming drug lord. With his pressed suit and spit polished shoes you could tell he is definitely trying to make an impression for the new suppliers. However he is the man with the necessary connections to secure the merchandise therefore he will control it, but he needs one thing – Scapatechi's money. This is where Scapatechi comes in. With his money and Francez's connections, the suppliers will see that they mean real business; however none of the two men trusted each other, due to past encounters.

Their main contact is known as 'The Dice'. Apparently the name suited him very well, as he would give his victims one last chance to live by using the throw of a dice to decide their fate. If they guess the number on the dice correctly, they would live! However, a one in six chance is not so good, but the way 'The Dice' saw, it was better than no chance at all.

Smartly dressed in a tailor fitted long black coat and his hair combed back as tight as he could get it 'The Dice' heads the meeting. With a calm voice he opens the meeting.

"Welcome gentlemen! I have brought to you a taste of what I can give you, the question is, are you willing to pay the price?" With his stare and his voice, you could tell there was no way he would say please, let alone give a receipt.

The drugs consist of a wide variety, all from the black-market of course, and mostly European. Amongst the various bags and cases, Scapatechi notices a black granite case.

'Kind of fancy for the occasion, I wonder what it is.' Scapatechi ponders to himself. The Dice catches his gaze.

"That's not with the deal!" States a voice with a tone that told you it wasn't up for discussion.

European suppliers had delivered this black case, and The Dice had plans to sell this to the upper end of the market, maybe the U.S. Government, an insider told him that he could reach a cool ten million for it.

The case contained a formula secretly developed by German military scientists during the Second World War, believed to enhance a human beings strength, speed and physique. Apparently Hitler's psychotic plan was to create the ultimate foot soldiers, but his military council was denied any chance to test or deploy the substance before their empire crumbled. Needless to say, it was incredibly valuable.

"I have been trying to get my hands on it for some time now," said a very cocky Mr Dice. He continues to brag about its history and value until he is swiftly cut off by a very sharp tongued Scapatechi,

"Enough of the pleasantries, let us just get down to f**king business shall we!" The Dice falls silent, somewhat shocked at Scapatechi's cutting outburst. He looks towards Carlos Francez, as if looking for an excuse, then back at Scapatechi. Just as The Dice was about to pipe up he was interrupted by Francez,

"I mean, I hate to agree with this guy, but business is business Mr Dice, this is New York buddy, not some European recreational club, bragging about how much of the world you think you own!

When Francez had finished his brave speech Scapatechi looks at him with a very surprised look on his face,

"I didn't think you had the balls Francez!" Scapatechi whispers from behind his hand,

"Neither did I." Francez mutters back. The two ruthless gangsters must have looked like a pair of mischievous schoolboys to The Dice.

You could have heard a pin drop until The Dice starts a low laugh. Scapatechi and Francez look at each other with a strange look of confusion, and then of course they start to laugh to. It doesn't take long for the noticeably fake laughter to stop, then the makeshift meeting house falls silent, a silence that is only broken by the sound of sirens which begins a few seconds later. Unknown to the gangsters, they are actually the sirens of the fire department responding to the call at the old apartment blocks.

"I've been double crossed!" The Dice shouts furiously. The Dice quickly opens fire on Scapatechi and Francez, resulting in pure pandemonium in the warehouse. With bullets flying everywhere, the gangsters take cover.

Scapatechi takes a hit on the shoulder, but manages to return fire; hitting The Dice twice in the chest sending him back against the cases of dirty money. As The Dice crashes to the ground his near lifeless hand releases two small red cubes. The two red cubes lay amongst a flutter of fifty dollar bills, Francez can't believe his luck,

"Two birds down and I didn't even through a stone," he cackles to himself whilst wiping a bead of sweat from his brow.

Making his way over to the now near paralysed Mr Dice, Francez looks down at the two red cubes which where partly covered by the flutter of fifties.

"Well, what have we here, a pair of sixes?" Francez laughs with a hint of sarcasm. However his laugh is cut short when he notices the barrel of a gun peeping out from under The Dice' blood drenched jacket,

"Guess again Francez," said the Dice with a quivering but direct voice. A second of silence feel, though to Francez it seems to last forever, when suddenly he feels a tingling sensation in his gut. The Dice had blasted Francez in the stomach sending him to his knees. Just before The Dice checks out he whispers to Frances,

"Snake eyes my friend. It is only then that a slight breeze from a broken window blows the fifty dollar bills from the two red cubes revealing a pair of ones. In Las Vegas a pair of ones is also known as 'snake eyes.'

Scapatechi lets out a yell caused by the bullet that is lodged in his left shoulder; he manages to pull himself to his feet before turning to Francez who is now doing his best to crawl to the nearest exit.

"Help…" moans a desperate Francez who feels his life slipping away inch by inch.

"You could have said please," mutters Scapatechi, his voice laced with derision. Seriously injured and near death, Francez reaches a weak arm out for help. Scapatechi lifts his gun and looks directly into Francez petrified eyes. Without sarcasm or even a second thought he drills Francez with led. Scapatechi falls silent, looking at the smoking barrel of his gun he contemplates what to do. He frantically gathers up what's left of the money and drugs which have been scattered about the warehouse as result of the gunfire.

Now shaking with an adrenalin rush Scapatechi takes a glance out a nearby window to see to his amazement that the sirens were not from police units wishing to bust the mob leaders, but from the fire department that are tending to an old apartment block fire?

5

A few hours earlier, Michael at home and alone stared into the gas flame of an old range oven in the kitchen, with that sick feeling in his gut telling him that Bill would be home soon. Time passed too quickly for Michael as he soon heard the faint sound of footsteps nearing the apartment door. Sure enough, it was Bill-drunk, violent, and as if to prove himself as a man, he started beating the living hell out of Michael as soon as he found his trusty old belt.

Whilst Bill was on his beating spree, Michael suddenly moved aside, causing an excessively aggressive Bill to loose his balance, flail wildly and fall to the ground slamming his head against the kitchen floor. A badly bleeding and bruised Michael took his chance to defend himself, doing so by reaching for the small fire extinguisher that was mounted near the gas oven. Using it with all the strength he could muster, he whacked his stepfather over the head. Bill dazed and confused struggled to his feet, though totally off balance. When he eventually pulled his limp body from the grimy tiled floor he was met with a sharp blow to the temple, the sheer force of the extinguisher sent him on top of the open range, straight onto the flames. Chaos ensues…

Seconds later, Caroline and Rachel return to the apartment, to their surprise they were met with the glow and roar of a now quickly spreading fire. Within seconds, the small apartment was engulfed with flames and filling the corridors with smoke. A shaky voice beyond the fire screamed,

"I'm sorry… He made me do it… He made me!"

"Jesus Michael! What on earth have you done?" His Mother shrieked

"C, Cough!" Spluttered Rachel, everyone knew that it was time to get out.

Neighbours in the apartment block heard the commotion, and were all witnesses to the quickly spreading fire. The alarm was raised and the Fire Department were quickly called. By now it was too late, the damage had already been done and the blaze continued to tear through the dingy old apartment block like dry woodland.

Quickly to arrive at the apartments, Mason and the team look for people, bodies, anything they can save. Due to the quick thinking and professionalism of the crew, they are swift in preparing for and entering the inferno. Mason hears the distant screams of a woman's voice.

"Help me, my Daughter is in there!" Caroline had lost Rachel on their way out of the apartment block due to the smoke and chaos; she was terrified of loosing her entire family to the flames, and is now yelling as hard as her lungs would allow her. Roaring into the carnage from the buildings entrance, she catches the attention of Mason, who finally moves in towards her.

"What floor ma'am?" He yells, however at this point Caroline is hysterical and not making any sense at all, blurting out random numbers…

"5th… 6th…"

"Come on, answer me!" Mason roars impatiently before placing his strong hands onto Caroline's shoulders.

"Now calm it lady, think!" A frantic Caroline begins to calm with the presence of Mason's voice and touch, her heavy breathing also begins to slow. She is entranced by Mason's eyes, and then softly mutters the words,

"The 4th floor…" Without wasting another second Mason is on the move, frantically leading the way to the fourth floor dodging falling debris and bursts of flames. Beyond the smoke filled corridors

Mason can just about make out a faint voice, a child's voice.

"Help me please!" A shaking Rachel coughs, who by now is lying on the floor beneath an old writing desk. Knowing that her next breath may be her last she almost gives up hope, when suddenly she sees a figure coming from beyond the smoke, gradually growing larger, like a giant from the shadows. However this was no giant, it was Mason Hope.

He picks up the girl's limp form and starts the journey back to safety, placing his own respirator mask on the girls face filling her lungs with clean air. In doing so he notices the incinerated carcass of a much charcoaled body, turning the girl's eyes away from the drastic vision he continues to move onward.

Finding little Rachel was one thing but getting the pair out alive would not be as easy as the apartment was now dancing with flames. As a brave Mason continues through the fire with the terrified girl clutched tightly in his arms he whispers into her ear.

"I won't let you go, I promise!" Still anticipating his next move he looks into the little girls eyes and as he does so he finds his daughter's strength deep inside her, and for an instant he gets lost in the moment.

Interrupted by the sound of a falling rafter beam, Mason quickly sharpens up and dashes out to the corridor; he looks to his left and through the smoke can just about notice the faint haze of a green exit sign. Without a moment to spare Mason covers Rachel with his fire jacket and makes a dash towards the light, dodging flames and leaping over burning carpet on the way. The exit door is swiftly dealt with by a heavy kick from his boot, sending the flaming oak doors crashing into the street four floors below.

Now safely outside the building Mason leans over Rachel, just as her eyes are opening she catches sight of the man who had just saved her life. Time seems to stand still for the two of them causing Rachel to forget the surrounding chaos and feel safe, a feeling she hasn't had in a long time. Mason had unforgettable eyes; Rachel knew that she would remember this man and that he would be in her dreams and memories forever.

Outside the smouldering apartment Mason and his crew get a chance to regroup. Although the guys have most of the residents out safe, including poor old Mrs Garbonee who is still gripping tightly to her mug of coffee, with her hair rolled up in huge rollers. Mason gives the order to do one final swoop to ensure the apartment block is clear, as they assume formation a fierce blast lights up the docks like a fireworks display, drawing everyone's attention to the ferocity of the inferno as it carries itself on to neighbouring buildings on the docks. One of which being the warehouse where Scapatechi and his business associates had their bloody deal gone wrong.

As the team battle the flames, a scorched and adrenaline filled Michael scrambles around the frantic crowds of firefighters and rescued tenants, while his mother Caroline is trying to brief the police on tonight's actions. Michael spots her and fearing the world of trouble he is now in, he runs off further down the docks, passing Mason and the team as he goes. Mason catches a glimpse of the boy scrambling into an old warehouse, realising it's only a matter of time before the warehouse catches fire he contemplates his next move.

"Guys," he shouts over the roar of the flames, and hiss of the water hose.

"A little kid just ran into the old warehouse over there, I need to get him before the whole place goes up!" Without waiting for a '*yeah Mason that sounds like a good idea,*' he leaves for the warehouse. His team continue their battle with the fire, rescuing as many as they physically can from the doomed apartment block.

Mason enters the warehouse, speedily manoeuvring himself from one side to the other. Dodging through rows of crates, he catches sight of the boy at the rear of the warehouse and makes his way towards him. Michael, from the corner of his eye sees the firefighter coming his way and fearing he is in big trouble he makes a dash to escape punishment. As Mason runs towards him, he glances back to find that the fire has already started eating its way into the side of the ramshackle warehouse. Knowing that time is against him, he makes a run in the direction of where he last saw the boy. He soon stops in his tracks when he is met with the visage of a mini massacre, with the bodies of The Dice and a very bloody Carlos Francez strewn on the dusty warehouse floor, mixed with bags of powder, tablets and all sorts Before he can even process what his eyes have encountered, there's a loud crash behind him. Turning instinctively to find the source of the sound, he sees two heavy burning rafters now blocking the entrance, which was also the only exit. The fierce blaze continues tearing its way through the warehouse as if it were old news paper. The old dry wooden crates make perfect kindling wood.

By now Scapatechi is safely outside albeit without his ill-gotten gains, and as the crazed gangster now looks back at the crime scene, he mutters to himself,

"So long losers, Ha Ha..."

Mean while inside the warehouse time is running out for Mason and the kid, battling heroically through the flames, Mason gets what may be his last chance to save both their lives.

'There you are!' Mason thinks into himself whilst grinding his teeth he notices the kid's shadow produced by the flaming glow of the ever creeping fire so he takes his chance and smashes his way through burning creates and clutches a struggling, wriggly Michael by the scruff of his neck. Swiftly moving towards a window at the edge of the warehouse, he throws Michael over his shoulder and begins to climb an old wooden ladder. As he nears the top, he sets the now semi-conscious kid on the ledge, while doing so he peers through the open window where he notices a man running from the warehouse with what seems to be bags of money. Mason reckons the guy must be in a rush as a flurry of notes fly from the bags as he runs.

"Stop…" Mason shouts; he just wanted the man to raise the alarm, to let his team know he was trapped at the window with their exit burnt to a cinder, but when the man turns around, their eyes suddenly meet. Putting two and two together Mason casts his mind back to the bloody bodies that lay on the ground. Scapatechi senses the firefighter's thoughts and gives him a chilling smile before continuing onwards into the shadows. Mason knew this man; this was the animal behind a lot of the city's violence. This was the man who a few years back torched a restaurant for the simple reason that the owner wouldn't pay protection money. Scapatechi being the cold heartless monster he was busted a bottle of bourbon against the side of the chef's head before setting the poor guy on fire. The way Scapatechi saw it, if they had of paid up, the chef would have been fine. It was Mason's crew that attended the scene that night, there were two innocent victims, Mason recalled.

Just then the ladder gave way; it broke the moment Mason had placed Michael safely on the outer window ledge causing him to fall to the floor with a thud. As he comes to, he notices the hot flames now surround him. Feeling dazed and confused, he staggers to his feet and with blurred vision can just about make out a black case on the floor in front of him. It was making unusual bubbling and gurgling noises, which was rather disconcerting. Just then, an outlandish blue mist floats and wafts towards him, filling his lungs with every short breath he takes. However before he can react, he inhales a great deal of the foreign vapour. Mason falls to his knees were he grips his throat and gasps for air, hanging on to consciousness with the little strength he has left.

High above Mason safely nestled on the window ledge Michael slowly awakes from his smoke induced slumber, and looks on from safety. He to inhales a small amount of the blue mist, but wasn't even aware enough to notice. Suddenly, at the side of the warehouse, a few propane tanks explode destroying everything in its path. The resulting explosion obliterates the remaining wall, before tossing like rag dolls the firefighter and boy onto the edge of the dock.

Scapatechi looks on from a safe distance, turning ideas over in his head.

"Holy Shit", he yells to himself.

"Could that firefighter of made it?"

"If so could he ID me in a police line?"

"Possibly grass on me?"

"Is he a liability?" Scapatechi doesn't deliberate for long. Approaching the now beaten, braised and bruised firefighter, Scapatechi stands over him with a gun; pondering if the brave firefighter has even survived the blast, then notices a flickering opening of his eyes. Barely conscious, Mason just makes out the words.

"Wrong place, wrong time Mr," before he knew it, Mason heard the shots.

Mason was hit twice in the chest before his limp and lifeless body was kicked from the dock into the cold dark waters below by Scapatechi's well polished shoe. The shock of hitting the icy cold water brings some alertness back to him. With whatever strength he has remaining, Mason manages to ascend his way to the surface, were he grasps onto a slimy rope which lucky for him is attached onto a nearby ledge under the docks. With his last burst of strength he slowly pulls himself onto it were he remains lifeless and cold.

6

The crew had started to wonder where Mason was, but were clueless about his situation as they had enough to worry about. By now the blaze was slowly being controlled and any remaining tenants were already rescued. They are understandably relieved that this evenings call out was a near success until they heard a hissing sound.

"Sounds like a cat!" One of the guys shouts. With all victims now at a safe distance the crew march into the cindered wreck to find what ever it was making the strange sound.

"I think it's coming from under here,"

"Under this steel panel," comes a shout from one of the guys. The strong man power of Mason's team works together to heave the heavy hot steel panel to one side, but to the crew's surprise the sound was not a helpless feline but the hiss of a busted gas line.

Now down by what is left of the warehouse, Scapatechi hears the sounds of police sirens near by, and can't help overhearing a voice stating that a boy is prime suspect for the blaze and must be brought in. At that moment Scapatechi hears a rustle among some debris, and to his astonishment he finds a half dead kid, Scapatechi assumes this is the boy the cops are hunting down, and being the anikist he is, Scapatechi, now with only a few seconds to spare, decides to grab the boy and shelter him from the law. He didn't know exactly why he did it, he felt he had to, insurance maybe? Just as Scapatechi finally disappears into the protection of shadows, a powerful explosion makes itself known by lighting up the entire area; the blinding bright light is closely followed by a thunderous vibration causing the ruthless mobster to loose his balance for a second.

Now at the hospital, Caroline and Rachel look on from a window at the flood of patients, all from the dockland fire, and all accompanied by police officers.

"Mom, where is Daddy and Michael?" Rachel softly asks whilst holding her chest, Caroline doesn't quite know how to answer her confused, beautiful daughter. Seconds later she reaches for Rachel's hand, griping it tightly before breaking down into tears.

"What is wrong Mom?" Rachel softly asks.

"Nothing my little one, everything will be ok," Caroline replies whilst bowing her head to engage in a prayer. The hospital is buzzing with people, all running around in a fluster. To the left are police officers taking statements, to the right patients are screaming for doctors who are already run off their feet trying to tend to the helpless victims. However even with this image embedding itself in Rachel's mind, somewhere inside her she feels a rush of compassion, and a feeling of hope. Noticing the faces of the shocked and terrified patients change when they are finally graced with a doctor's presence was overwhelming for her. It is at this exact moment that she discovers her passion to help; to bring joy and not sorrow, and a willingness to change just a little piece of the world by doing something good, maybe getting her chance to be a part of the city of dreams along the way.

A Detective by the name of Frank Lombardo manoeuvres his way through the chaos like a man on a mission. His aim is to question Caroline Woods about a few things. Namely her husband's death, the whereabouts of her missing son and how the hell that fire had started. Lombardo also wants to explain to Caroline that the firefighter that saved her little girl is still MIA (missing in action), and presumed dead.

"Woods, Caroline Woods... Have you seen her?" The Detective forcefully asks a young nurse.

"I think the Woods family are over there, just beyond the water fountain." The young nurse replies, she is quite startled from the Detectives boisterous demands but co-operates fully before moving along.

Not far from the hospital, laid beneath the old docking bay, an extremely pain filled Mason comes to, with his head pounding and his heart racing, he feels every muscle in his body burning, as if he is being incinerated from the inside, followed by excruciating razor sharp bolts of pain that spread throughout his tensed body like a wild fire; being shot twice in the chest didn't help matters either.

As this feeling continues to take control of his body, his hands grow, his fists turn block like and Mason can do nothing but scream with the sheer agony of it, with thoughts of his fate spinning over and over in his mind.

A man apart

Now dropping on one knee with his arms reaching out for two nearby wooden posts to grip tightly he tries to fight the effects of the foreign chemicals, though is powerless to stop it. His shoulders and arms grow, causing his coat to stretch across his back showing excessive muscular detail beneath the wet and worn fire jacket. As his legs develop and swell the wooden planks beneath him bow with the pressure of his ever increasing mass. His mind turns over a thousand thoughts all at once; it's as if his whole life is flashing in front of his eyes. Nearing the end of this mesmerizing transformation, he throws his head back and lets out a large yell causing his teeth to grind as his throat muscles being to contract. With a struggle to cry out, Mason frustratingly can barely even muster a groan, in effect causing him to slump to the ground with a heavy thud. As he lies on the wet musky planks, a damp smell of harbour water begins to ventilating his nostrils causing him to feel even more nauseous. Determined to survive he tries once more to call out for help, after a short weak murmur passes his lips the firefighter crashes to his knees and falls forward where he lays until his sight was nothing more than blackness.

7

He awakes. It seems like days have past. 'Was it a dream?' He wonders. Mason staggers to his feet, still a little dazed, but after a few seconds he begins to focus.

"Where the hell am I?" He mutters to himself.

"Am I dead?"

"Is this hell?" A flashback of the past few hours events give him an unkind reminder like a blow to the head. He finally remembers. As he pulls himself to higher ground, still a little off balance, his legs immediately buckle from under him, once more sending him to his knees with a crunch. With his full weight now on his hands he feels a fiery sensation on his chest causing him excruciating pain. As he learns to accept the pain he begins to focus.

"Breath God dam it, breath!" Mason Pants, whilst placing pressure on his wounded chest. Looking upon the wooden planks below, he notices blood seeping from his wounds. Once again he envisions the shadow of a man standing over him with a gun.

"Scapatechi…" He remembers with a feeling of revenge. Slowly lifting his eyes Mason looks around for a few seconds where he analyses his surroundings, he quickly begins his ascent to the dock above were he gazes over towards the scene of the apartment fire. As only a little smoke on burnt debris remains Mason senses the feeling of lost time, as to him it only feels like a few minutes since he had arrived at the scene.

"The guys must have left hours ago!" He assures himself whilst looking at his wrist, were his watch should be; only stopping momentarily as he notices his hands.

"They're not my hands," he whispers with a low gruff voice. He then slowly touches his face.

"My God…"

"This can't be."

"I've got to get my ass back to the station," he tells himself. He knew he needs to be with people he can trust right now and that the old station seems like his only option.

Making his way towards the old station, he keeps to the shadows, not yet knowing what he has become, and not wanting to be subjected to the public eye he keeps a low profile. Still shaken, afraid, and looking for answers he continues to make his way towards familiar ground he cuts through the back streets and alleys were he crosses paths with a loan street drinker. The drunkard who was commonly known as Brad, with his moth eaten clothes and his shabby white hair, Brad was renowned for his crazy stories of U.F.O's and encounters with men in black. He had even claimed that he had found the famous 'Bigfoot'. Brad follows the firefighter with his eyes and watches on as this huge man passes under the blanket of shadows cast by the bright moon light. Mason returns a watchful eye to Brad as he still steadily moves forward until a turning car casts its head lamps down the ally for a mere second before speeding off in the opposite direction. The second of light was enough for Brad to catch a sharp glimpse of this mysterious firefighter, but when he rubs his eyes and scans the ally for another look he finds that he is alone.

"I've really got to cut down on this stuff!" Brad hick-ups to him self before studying his bottle of cheap wine.

"Not before I finish you off my beauty," he slurs to himself with a smile before pinning the bottle to his lips.

Finally nearing the old station Mason is met with police lights and officers taking statements from Dale.

'Where are the guys?' Mason ponders to himself. The sheer sight of all the lights and commotion stops him in his tracks, leaving him no other option but to watch on from behind a dumpster in an ally about twenty yards away.

Exhausted and confused he drops to his knees, with his head bowed, he opens his eyes and stares at his moonlit reflection in a puddle of water.

"What am I?" He whispers whilst touching his face again to prove that he isn't insane, to prove it's real. It is at this moment he decides to keep hidden from the police and wait for the guys to return. Knowing the final shift was nearing an end and that the station would be empty soon, he decided to wait for that window of time with them. He waits in the alley, in the shadows. Time seems to slow down and with his body still feeling on fire, he drifts off once more.

The roaring sound of an engine starting wakes him abruptly.

"I must have drifted off." Mason mutters as he rubs his eyes still a little drowsy. It was the sound of the vehicles leaving the station. In agony Mason rises to his feet to make his way over to the rear of the station. Still lurking in the shadows, in fear of being seen he runs around back to find the rear steel door is bolted shut, but undeterred,

Mason pulls at the door handle twisting the door from it's hinges as if it were made from aluminium. Already stunned by this show of strength, he then manages to throw the heavy steel door from him like any of us would throw a piece of paper into a trashcan. He looks at his hands in total shock and astonishment whilst thinking to him self.

'I don't think this is one of those dreams were I am going to be woke up with breakfast in bed!' Just before he enters the station a stray alley cat jumps out from behind a few creates causing him to yell out,

"Jesus! What the…" He shrieks as he watches the alley cat as it makes its way off into the darkness.

"Go on, get out of here!" Mason growls whilst wiping the sweat from his brow with his sleeve.

8

Standing alone, peering into the dark empty station, Mason enters and walks around for a few minutes. It doesn't take him long to realises the place is empty, as the echo of his footsteps sounds throughout the room. A feeling of abandonment falls over Mason as he himself feels empty like the station. Once a warm building full of feeling and honour now feels cold and lifeless, for him the station is now only an empty void, no one to help him or to trust. It is a moment of harsh reality. A few eerie moments pass before Mason decides to priorities his direction towards his family, to ensure their safety; he swiftly grabs his jeep keys from the rack and franticly heads towards the door. Before he can even reach it, a chilling voice from the shadows shouts out,

"Who goes there?" Mason ducks down, shielding himself behind the nearest bench he can find, until the voice repeats it's self, but this time there is strength in the words.

"I heard you… Who goes there?" Mason knows the voice, but due to his current state of mind he just can't place it.

An eerie silence falls between the two men, leaving an echoing chill in the room. Before another word is spoken Mason makes a dash for the exit door. He manages about four steps then to his amazement, as if from nowhere, the mysterious man confronts him wielding an axe. The two men both scream at each other, both scared witless soon stop in their tracks.

Mason swiftly removes the axe from the man with such ease he surprises even himself. Due to the limited lighting, only the silhouettes of the two men are visible. Mason's silhouette looks shockingly monstrous and causes the other guy to shake with pure horror. To Mason's surprise, the mysterious man from the shadows, who's identity was revealed only by him stepping into a ray of moonlight is none other than Dale. As Dale had really no family, the station officers, with the State of New York appointed Dale to maintain the station. They knew of his passion for the building and the importance of having a man they could trust maintain the building. However Dale kept this information from the guys.

Dale, rendered speechless with shock, stutters nonsense as the impostor towers over him.

"Dale, it's me!" Mason ventures. As he steps into the pale moonlight, Dale takes a few steps back, wondering how this man knows him. Then suddenly it came to him.

"Hang on, those eyes, it can't be."

"Mason, is that you?" Dale stammers whilst adjusting his glasses.

The two men, still in total shock and disbelief, try to understand what has happened.

"My God Mason, what the hell happened to you?" Dale finally musters the courage to ask. Dale is mesmerised, he cannot find the words or the thought to comprehend what is happening before him. Mason decides to give Dale a few more minutes before relaying the night's events to him, from the callout right up to the bodies and explosion. Dale can't believe what he is hearing, or in fact what he is seeing. The sight of Mason's appearance makes him feel very emotional, as he can't believe that this huge man before him was once his friend and colleague.

"It's still me Dale, somewhere in here at least," reasons Mason's extremely course and rough voice. Knowing the sheer sight of him makes Dale feel uneasy Mason decides to step back into the shadows were he remains.

"Ah, how are the guys?" Mason asks with an anxious tone. Dale hesitates to answer.

"Answer me!" Mason shouts, his voice startling Dale more than intended, Hell, it even startles Mason.

"I asked you a question! How are they?" He persists. Dale doesn't know how to break the news to Mason.

"They're gone!" Dale whimpers, his voice trailing off. This isn't enough for Mason so he continues to press Dale for answers.

"I know they were on call Dale! But were there any injuries?" Dale still hadn't worked out how best to put it to the now fiery giant.

"I mean they're gone Mason, I am sorry. Lombardo delivered the news to me himself, he said that you were feared dead too, that being the reason why they went into the building looking for you, when there was another explosion, more propane tanks or a gas line, they're still not sure."

"They're all gone!" Dale just lets it all out at once. Mason doesn't accept the news at first, staring Dale square in the eyes to find out the truth. He knows that Dale wouldn't lie but didn't want to believe him either. Stepping from the shadows, Mason cries out a heart wrenching 'NO...' Whilst slamming his two block like fists down against the workbench, leaving two massive dents on the surface. Seconds later he lets out another huge cry, this time slamming his fists down until the workbench couldn't take anymore, causing it to crumble into dust. Mason buries his head in his hands as he sobs.

"My fault, it's all my fault." He was always there for the guys. This time wasn't supposed to be any different.

"No Mason, it wasn't your fault!" Dale firmly states, although he himself can't help but feel sorry for the big guy. When Dale moves closer to Mason, he notices blood.

"My God Mason, you're bleeding!" Mason recalls Scapatechi and the shooting, but only chilling flashbacks.

"Let's get a look at you!" Dale offers in a comforting, sympathetic tone. Dale leads Mason out to the main workshop and frantically starts clearing his large cold steel bench.

"Jesus Dale, did you ever think about hiring a cleaner!" Mason suggests with a smile.

"Yeah sure Mason, now take off your shirt and climb up on this bench for me." Dale orders, whist rummaging around in his tool kit for a pair of long nose pliers. "These ought to do the trick." Dale says to himself whilst reaching for his hip flask.

"Surely now is not the time for that Dale." Mason questions.

"Of course not, I'm sterilising the instrument!" Dale replies as he pours the whiskey over the end of the pliers. Then when Mason's is turned Dale pins the hip flask to his mouth to calm his nerves. With Mason's shirt removed, Dale is able to spot the two bullet holes that Scapatechi gladly gave him.

"Jesus, Mason you've been shot! Do you not feel that?" Dale stammers whilst looking Mason in the eyes.

"I feel nothing," Mason replies. Dale ignores Mason's words then raises the pair of long nosed pliers and continues to find and pull the bullets from Mason's chest. Mason looks on in horror as Dale is probing his wounds with these so called medical tools.

"Hold on a minute, before you even move another inch!" Mason shouts.

"What is it Mason, does it hurt?" Dale replies in a concerned manor.

"Just hand me that hip flask of yours Dale." Mason asks with his now large but trembling hand reaching out.

"Yeah of course you can, there is plenty in there." Dale looks on as Mason finish it all. Dale looks at the empty hip flask while turning it upside down, then gives Mason a look. At that Dale continues to muster around in Mason's chest.

"I think I found one." Dale shrieks with a tone of achievement.

Mason doesn't even flinch. It was as if he felt nothing, as Dale drops the bullet into a near by dish. It doesn't take him long to retrieve the other bullet as Scapatechi had grouped them well.

"I'm going to get some air that was intense." Dale states as he makes his way to the rear of the station to clear his head and gather his thoughts. Mason, still looking at his hands, stands up from the bench and walks over to a large wall-mounted mirror; Dale always said it made the room look bigger, but everybody knew that Dale liked to pose a lot; well that was the joke anyway. As Mason looks at himself in the mirror, the only thought that comes into his head is,

'What the hell am I?'

Despite having two bullets removed from his chest, Mason feels physically superior. He looks above him were he notices an iron support beam, he jumps straight up about two feet and grasps onto the beam were he pulls his body up with ease. He manages an easy ten pull-ups before dropping down again with a heavy thud, causing the ground to shake. When the dust settles he cracks his neck from side to side relieving some tension when he notices a group picture of his team mounted on the wall. Lifting it down from the red bricked wall, Mason notices that the picture looks so small in his huge hand. It was too much to bear. The strain of seeing his now deceased comrades takes its toll on Mason, as he lashes out by clenching his fist and pounds it into a nearby wall leaving quite a hole. Opening the hand where the picture was once cradled, shards of glass remain lodged in his palm causing his hand to bleed.

"There blood is on your hands now alright," he tells himself, now deeply depressed.

Making his way to the rear of the station, Mason continues to look around reminiscing and absorbing the sounds and the smells of the place still thinking of his team.

"Jesus, why did this happen?"

"Why them?"

"They were good guys!"

Mason contemplates in despair.

"There is no purpose or reason in blaming yourself Mason; it really wasn't your fault." Reassures the now returning Dale in the most convincing voice he can muster.

"I should have been with them Dale, I wouldn't have let them go back in alone!" Mason counters.

"They were my friends too Mason! How do you think I feel?" Dale exclaims in a furious tone, causing Mason to fall silent.

Dale regarded these men as his family and hearing of their deaths was as if someone had ripped his heart out.

"Look Mason, I'm sorry but right now you're all I have left in the world." Dale tells him with real feeling.

"What about me Dale?"

"What about my family?"

"They think that I am dead!"

"What about my life?" Mason retorts emotionally before storming out of the old station, with only one destination in mind, home.

A series of red and blue lights lit up the room, waking Amanda from her sleep. They startle her at first but the more she comes to, the worse the feeling in her gut becomes. Deep down she knows something is wrong. She speedily gets out of bed and puts on her robe and hastily makes her way into Tyler's bedroom.

"Mom, is that Dad home?" A sleepy Tyler murmurs whilst rubbing his eyes.

"I don't know Son, I don't know." Amanda replies with a blank look in her eyes. Just as the police cars arrive at his home, Mason arrives almost simultaneously, stopping just beyond a tree across the street where he remains under the protection of darkness. Watching from a safe distance, he witnesses his wife Amanda answer the front door to the awaiting police men. The officers remove their caps when breaking the news of her husband's accident, then seconds later Mason notices his heartbroken wife breaking down in floods of tears. Accompanying the officers was detective Frank Lombardo. He had been the detective who had broke the news of Lydia's death a few years back, it must have been like hell all over again for poor Amanda when she saw Lombardo at the front door. Moments later, Tyler runs to the door, pausing for a second before comforting his Mother, by doing what he thought would feel best, hugging her tightly.

Frustrated and helpless Mason can do nothing but stand in the shadows, as he watches their hearts break in front of his eyes. Mason's heart slows; if you listen close enough you could almost hear it break. He has seen enough. Mason Hope, a man who for years fought his way through dangerous walls of flames, giving people a second chance of life, has now lost every thing he ever loved due to the sacrifices he's made for others. Backing off into the shadows with the blood from his heavy heart draining, a feeling of emptiness takes over. Just as his face retreats into the uninviting blackness, a tear falls from his piercing blue eyes.

Lombardo hears a rustle behind him, and pivots round quickly.

"What is it boss?" One of the officers asks hesitantly.

"Shhh…" Lombardo stresses as he strains to look into the shadows for movement.

"What the… Is that a person?" He isn't sure. He can just about make out a large; make that very large, black silhouette in the distance. Just as he is about to motion an officer to investigate, the outline seems to blend in with the darkness and whatever it was; was gone. Deciding he didn't want to take any insanity tests back at the precinct, he chooses to keep to himself what he had just witnessed.

9

A beautiful marble memorial monument glistens in the morning sun. The rays of sunlight are like ladders from heaven, as if, for the fallen firefighters to climb. Their stars-and-stripe laden coffins are brought to the burial site one by one. They are lined up beside one another, just like one final roll call.

The burial ceremony begins with an old preacher's preaching's.

"And on to heaven you shall go, for is now your time, though you Blue Angles will be remembered forever." The preacher's words give at least some comfort to the families. Mason watches on from a distance. As the names are read out by the old preacher, a chilling silence falls over the memorial site. The only sounds heard of a loan piper playing.

Through it all the preacher bravely continues, unperturbed. Tyler knows deep down in his heart that these men before him including his Dad died for a purpose, they are all heroes to him and indeed to the city, that was the only thing keeping him from breaking down, him knowing they will be remembered forever. Tyler casts his mind back and recalls his old man saying once, that the greatest feeling you could ever have is saving a life…

✳✳✳

"Son, come out here for a few seconds." Mason called to Tyler who was sitting happily watching cartoons.

"Dad, I'm busy! Can't it wait?" Tyler replied while munching on a chocolate chip cookie.

Mason entered the house and called again.

"Come on Son, I need a little help out here."

"Help'what kind of help Dad." Tyler questioned with a puzzled look, not wanting to do any more chores he lay on the couch pretending to be ill.

"Well Son, I was kind of hoping you could help me with a little fire fighting job." Mason said with a disappointing tone, and then continued…

"Oh well, if you're really not feeling very well, I will just have to go do it all by myself."

Tyler's eyes lit up when he heard the words *'fire fighting job'* and with in a few seconds he was on his feet.

"Wait a minute Dad; you didn't say anything about a fire fighting job!" Tyler spouted, while putting on his converse all stars.

"I just did Son, I'll ah, meet you out back when your ready." Mason replied with a compromising voice.

When Tyler finally pulled himself together he made his way out to the back yard were he saw his father standing by the fence talking to the neighbour Old Mr Peabody. Mr Peabody had called for a little professional help.

"Well Dad, what is this emergency you needed help with, or are you just tricking me into painting the fence again." Tyler asked in a sarcastic tone, whilst looking at the fence in suspicion. Mason walked over to Tyler and knelt down in front of him,

"Take a look up the tree Son, just over my shoulder." Mason requested. Tyler had followed his Dad's request, and just as he gazed up into the tree were he noticed the familiar image of the neighbours dog. Rex was a stereotype Yorkshire terrier, small, annoying and extremely noisy. His bark was worse than his bite though. Rex was Mr Peabody's pride and joy; he was all he had after Mrs Peabody passed away. Nobody ever knew how Rex did it, but every so often that crazy dog would have ended up in Mr Peabody's tree. Unbelievable, who ever heard of a climbing Yorkshire terrier?

"Well are you going to save Rex or not, young firefighter Tyler?" Old man Peabody echoed across the fence startling him. Then Mason gave Tyler a wink.

"Go on son, this one is all yours."

Tyler looked at his Dad with anticipation and then over to old man Peabody.

"Well Sir, what seems to be the trouble?" Tyler asked in a professional manor. Mason looked on proudly then walked across the yard to the patio to find a seat, only after giving old Peabody a nod of thanks.

"Well young man, it's my dog you see, he seems to be trapped up this tree, can you help at all?" Peabody asks Tyler in a noticeably fake stressful tone. However to Tyler's ears this was great, someone actually needing his help, he recalled an overwhelming feeling of importance, which gave him the confidence he needed.

"Sure Sir, just let me get my ladder." Tyler replied while still analysing the situation.

"Thanks young man, that will be just dandy, I will be out in a jiffy boy, weak bladder you know." Mr Peabody shouted across the fence before waddling into the house, holding his crotch. Tyler now stood alone at the foot of the tree staring up at Rex.

✳✳✳

The preacher's last words startle Tyler, bringing his mind back to the present,

"Ashes to ashes… Dust to dust… Amen." Tyler bows his head, then a whisper.

"Amen."

The ceremony comes to a close with griping the hearts and tear pockets of their left loved ones; Including Amanda who is lost in a trance. They listen on to the preacher's final words whilst holding each other tightly.

Off in the distance Mason lifts his head and notices that Tyler is standing over his coffin. He leaves something on it, but Mason is unable to make out what it is. As the mourners begin to silently walk away from the site Mason also notices one man that stays behind. It is Dale, staring straight at where Mason is standing, or perhaps even farther. They had a mutual feeling of loss, an unwritten understanding and empathy. Giving Mason a knowing nod Dale walks away, leaving Mason alone, knowing that he will wish to say his own personal goodbyes.

After making his way towards the caskets, Mason stands before the headstone with a terrible feeling of guilt and loss. He places his hand on the names which will be embedded forever in this block; he notices his own name carved on the cold marble along side the other Blue Angels. Looking down onto his own empty casket he spots what Tyler had left with him. It was the kid's baseball and mitt, perhaps Tyler's most cherished possession. Mason lifts the mitt and places it in the pocket of his coat.

Before walking away Mason kneels down on one knee before the central monument, paying his fallen comrades, one final honourable farewell. As he kneels there in the silence a heavy shower of rain begins to fall beating heavy off the ground and soaking Mason through and through. Undeterred, Mason holds his position until he is truly ready to let go.

10

A roaring fire lights up the room were a half dead kids lies on a bed. Two dark figures share his presence.

"Can you fix him doc?" One of the men asks in a concerned tone.

"The boy is in pretty bad shape Mr Scapatechi; I'll give him a shot, however I can't promise you anything." The Doctor replies as he lifts a syringe into the fire light whilst peering into it before squeezing the bubbles out. Scapatechi looks on as the Doctor injects the boy in the left shoulder.

"Give him time to rest, maybe six to eight hours and if there is no change, well..." The Doctor pauses briefly before bowing his head.

"Thank you Doc, thank you." Scapatechi mutters as he reaches into his jacket pocket before producing a cigar.

"I'll walk you out." Scapatechi offers as he rummages around in his other pocket trying to find his matches.

"It's no trouble, I know the way." The doctor replies closing his brown leather case.

The Doctor makes his way towards the dark mahogany door were he stops and waits for it to open. The door man acknowledges the Doctor as he passes through and peers into the fire lit bedroom for a few seconds before closing the door once more.

'What the hell am I doing?' Scapatechi thinks to him self as he looks on at the boy still trying to find his matches.

Turning his back to the boy Scapatechi frantically looks upon the mantle piece then the hearth.

"Jesus, were the hell is all the God dam matches!" He shouts his voice now a little deeper. During his frantic search he senses a watch full eye causing him to fall still. Slowly turning around Scapatechi notices a shadow, a shadow not cast by the fire light but from something else.

Still slowly pivoting around Scapatechi is met with the boy's dark eyes, the boys face is glowing, glowing from the fire which he holds in his hand.

"What the..." Scapatechi gasps with total shock before dropping his cigar on the floor.

"What, what..." Scapatechi can't find the words he wishes to speak; there are so many things he wants to ask.

"What's...? What is your name boy?" Still mesmerised by the fascinating gift the boy produces, Scapatechi can only think of how he can use him.

"My name..." The strange boy whispers under his breath. Just then a heavy knock sounds from the mahogany door.

"Not now, not now you fool!" Scapatechi roars to the anxious doorman, however the knock continues.

"What the hell do you want?"

"Who is it?" Scapatechi demands with little patients.

"It's the police sir; they want to ask you a few questions." The doorman mutters.

"Send them down to my office; I'll be there in a few minutes." Scapatechi answers in a calm voice; he always knew how to react around cops, calm and dumb.

Looking back towards the boy, Scapatechi places his hand on his head and whispers,

"Sleep now for you will need your strength... Flynt." Before making his way to the door he lifts his cigar and puts it back into his jacket pocket when he discovers the box of matches beneath the central card table.

"Ha… Would you look at that he says to Flynt before throwing him a wink and a smile. A frighteningly confused Michael watches on as his newly adopted father leaves the room, the sudden thud of the mahogany door causes his to jump, though deep down he senses a feeling of security in the warmth of the Dragon's lair.

11

Mason is sitting in front of the roaring fire at the old station; once again he turns and pours himself a scotch.

"It was just another Friday morning when we got the call, it was a car accident just off Bleeker Street; we never thought much of it at the time, until I noticed the little yellow school bus." Mason calmly relays the memory to Dale. Dale listens on with a heart felt look. He knew Mason held this story in a dark hidden place within his mind.

***

The fire crew swiftly arrived at the scene. To Mason's horror the mangled school bus was startlingly familiar.

"Jesus, Lydia!" He gasped as realisation hit. Mason knew deep down in his gut that the carnage before him was his daughter's school bus. Suddenly something in his mind snapped and at that moment he found himself in an uncontrollable passionate gallop heading towards the wreck. Spotted by Lombardo who then ordered his officers not to let this wild firefighter through, however Mason tried relentlessly to fight his way to the bus but was stopped in his tracks.

"Get the hell out of my way," wrestled Mason with grit determination.

"Sir we have orders not to let you through," comes a shout from one of the officers who was being pined to the ground by a very furious Dad.

"My Daughter's in there! He screamed!

"MY DAUGHTER'S IN THERE!!!"

✳✳✳

Breathing heavy, the memory seems to be too much for Mason at this time. Quickly topping up his glass with the rich malt scotch he raises his glass and whispers,

"Here's to them…"

"Yeah, to everyone we have ever lost." Dale echoes; now standing at the door.

They barely had their glasses to their lips before the red warning beacons in the station start to flash.

"What the hell…" Exclaims Mason; nearly spilling his drink.

"That's an emergency Mason! I cut the bell; thought there was no need any more," says a now exasperated Dale. Mason suddenly feels that familiar rush of adrenalin run through his veins. He jumps to his feet, and stresses,

"It's my duty Dale!" Dale looks at the red beckons then back towards Mason.

"Easy Mason, It's not your place no more, you can't be seen out like this!"

"Not anymore!" Dale protests; still trying not to sound negative.

"The hell I can't, the hell I can't!" Mason shouts in an agitated mood.

"Ok Mason, ok…" Dale backs down. He knows all to well that look in Mason's eyes. He's definitely the same guy inside all right, extremely dedicated.

"Ok, ok… I've got something for you Mason." Dale sighs in a defeated voice. Again an uneasy silence falls between them before Dale asks Mason to wait for a moment before walking towards his workshop. The big guy manages a half smile.

Moments later the wood slat double doors open to reveal a valiant firefighter complete with upgraded attire. Greater durability, with concealing properties, his helmet hides his face from view. Red braces line a tight white vest, presenting his muscular form at its fullest. A full length dark dusty brown firefighter's jacket completes the awesome appearance the sight of which sends shivers up Dale's spine as he looks on from the hanger.

A true American hero emerges from the darkness stepping into the light. The firefighter is truly reborn. He has nothing to lose, making it his sole purpose to stop the evil that tears through the city like poison in the veins of a pure body. Stopping at nothing to protect the innocent and the helpless, he will give courage and honour to those who deserve it, and hope to those who need it.

Mason's epic form fills the doors of the old station. Catching his eye, an orange glow lights up the skyline like an autumn sunrise. Just as he makes a move towards his primary goal, a wailing sound to his left grabs his attention.

"What the…" Mason questions. To his surprise it is a little ginger and white kitten stuck at the top of a nearby tree. In his low gruff voice Mason slowly whispers,

"You've got to be kidding me!"

New hope on the horizon

Nothing withstands his grit and determination to get to the fire scene, not even the hasty rescue of a small kitten. He bounds from rooftop to rooftop, using fists and axe to obliterate obstacles, undeterred of the great heights he leaps over. He ploughs onward, knowing that ever second is vital.

When he arrives at the scene, he first of all notices that the nearby Fire Department hasn't yet arrived. Without a moment to spare he enters the building from the top rapidly scouting each floor for survivors and victims. Anyone lucky or unlucky enough to be there would be thrown aloft his massive shoulders with ease. Thankfully the building was closed for renovations. However some pushy foreman had three of his workers on site day and night to finish the overdue job. It was really very much a bad coincidence.

"Help us… We're trapped!" Come the petrified screams of night workers catching Mason's attention,

"Hang in there!" Mason's loud roar echoes; the sheer velocity of which shocked the hell out of the already frightened workers causing them to look at each other with a look of horror. Not knowing now what to expect they continue screaming for help.

The workers now fearing the worst hold on for grim death as they hear and feel the thudding vibrations which continue to get louder. Suddenly the wall opposite the workers comes crashing down, but to their disbelief, instead of hot smouldering flames, they are met by the vision of a mysterious loan firefighter.

"Jesus… What the hell are you?" One of the quivering workers blurts out. Mason, unresponsive to the workers questions and screams as he has more important answers to find, like how the hell he was going to get them all out alive.

Throwing a worker on each shoulder and another under his arm Mason dashes frantically over to the now empty elevator shaft, where he fastens each of the workers to the harness beneath his jacket. Clutching tightly to the extremely coarse twisted steel elevator cable he thrusts himself down the shaft at an uncontrollable speed scaring the crap out of the workers before slamming into the ground floor where his boots leave two large dents in the concrete. Mason exits the building, with every soul he found carried to safety. Laying them on the sidewalk next to a family of Chinese tourists who are standing mesmerised at the explosive fire in front of them.

"I hope the overtime was worth it guys!" Mason calmly states to the workers with a look of sincerity.

The sound of a fire engines siren swiftly approaching catches his attention. All that was left was the blaze, having seconds to spare Mason decides to lend one final helping hand doing so by frantically searching along the sidewalk until he spots it.

"There you are." He mutters to himself. With one swipe of his axe, a nearby fire hydrant explodes like an expensive bottle of champagne and the water gushes wildly up into the air. Using both hands, Mason manages to grab the metal hydrant and twist it towards the direction of the fire, slowly but surely it becomes effective. Police and fire crews arrive at the scene just as one of the Chinese kids clicks off a few more snaps with his camera.

Mason now slips into the safety of darkness, to avoid contact with the local P.D. Needless to say, they are baffled at what Mason has left for them.

Stopping about three blocks away, Mason places both hands against a wall and leans into it trying to catch his breath. Not only did he deal with the fire but he had to run away too! Mason chuckles to himself.

"Ha, did you see the faces on that Chinese family…" Mason, for a moment, enjoys the irony of it all. It lasts a mere few seconds before he reminds himself of the fallen men who could have been with him. Straightening himself up, Mason sets off for home.

Making his way round to the rear of the station, Mason is met by sound of screeching tyres and blinding lights.

"Jesus… They've followed me!" Mason panics while he backs into the corner wielding his axe.

"Easy big guy, it's only Lombardo!" Dale shout's from the doorway. However, distressed by the situation and still dazzled by the lights, Mason thrusts his axe into the headlamps of the vehicle creating darkness once more; while Dale ducks down to avoid the flying sparks.

Inside the car Detective Lombardo looks on in astonishment,

"What the… Dale! Who the hell is this guy?" Lombardo now jumps from the car careering towards Dale yet keeping good distance from this mysterious firefighter. Lombardo, now hysterical, pushes Dale and himself into the station, causing them to fall to the ground with a rattle. Both men lie on the ground gazing out at the open door way at the moon light shining through producing a monstrous silhouette.

"Lombardo… Why didn't you say so?" Mason sarcastically comments with his course rough voice. Right then Lombardo's eyes roll up towards his brow weakly muttering,

"M-m-ason?" Followed by a very predictably loss of consciousness.

"For Heaven's sake Mason, Lombardo's out cold!"

"You scared the hell out of him!" Dale stutters whilst slapping Lombardo on each cheek; Mason looks on with a half smile, shrugging his shoulders.

12

Years later, a blue Mustang cruises into the city with some good music coming from the stereo. The young driver taps his hand in time to the beat and thinks to himself,

'Nothings changed much around here.' He cannot help but smile as he passes through the old neighbourhood he grew up in. Reminiscing about the old times, he mutters to himself.

"Where does the time go?" Finally reaching his destination, a Fire House located on 52nd Street, he pulls up and notices a group of young firefighters looking over at him, they mutter amongst themselves for a moment before deciding to make the move to meet and greet him, a mysterious young stranger. Stepping out of his car the young man stands tall with his bag on his shoulder soaking up the atmosphere of his new home, the sounds, the smells, he loves everything about it! He continues onwards towards engine one, when one of the guys makes a move to meet him half way.

Breaking the silence was a hot shot proby barely out of his probationary period; he went by the name off JJ. The hot shot calls across the yard.

"Yo… my names Jack Selinski, but my friends call me JJ." The young stranger gives JJ a nod of acknowledgment then extends his arm in search of a friendly handshake,

"Firm shake you got there…" JJ pauses briefly waiting for the new guy to give his name, but he does not, forcing JJ to continue the introductions.

"This here to my right is Kastle, and ah… Over there by the phone is Ding and over there at engine two is the Torelli brothers." The young man remembers his manners.

"Pleased to meet you guys." He responds looking extremely confident. Just as the handshakes had all finished another firefighter slides down the pole behind them, to the young mans surprise, it's a girl. She comes straight over, and with confidence says,

"So JJ, are you going to introduce me to the new guy, or are you going to just stand there looking at my chest?"

The only girl at that Fire House, Sandy could hold her own. She was pretty, but a tomboy through and through. As if to prove it, she is head of mechanical maintenance; needless to say, she definitely had this crew on the end of her leash.

"Sure! Pleased to meet you all, seriously, it's definitely an honour." The young man says with a knowing smile. Introductions over he reports to the station officer.

"New guy... Reporting for duty... Sir," the young man says with a disciplined voice.

"Ease up kid." Officer Goodall replies before pouring himself a fresh cup of coffee. This kind of broke the ice a little for young man as he was nervous enough about his transfer; however an older man, Goodall was a veteran of the service. He greets the young man warmly.

"Welcome aboard son, glad you could join our team!" He says, meaning every word.

"You are very punctual, I like that kid." The young man gazes on at officer Goodall admiring his discipline and love for the department. Goodall stood over six feet tall with short blonde wiry hair, though now going slightly grey, his voice was deep though extremely comforting. With a sudden interruption the welcoming atmosphere is disturbed by a sharp knock on the door. Without even waiting for a reply or consent, JJ opens the door and hurriedly says.

"You've really got to see this sir..." Goodall understood the tone.

"I will be right back Son, just wait here a moment, make yourself at home."

As Goodall had left with JJ, the young man took the opportunity to look around the office. He couldn't believe all the medals, accolades and regalia dedicated to officer Goodall decorating the walls. It was impressive,

'He certainly is a brave man,' the young stranger thinks to himself. However as overwhelming as all the medals were, it was the harrowing words of a faded newspaper cutting that caught his eye. It read,

"Mysterious phantom firefighter spotted at city blaze." The print was quite small, so the young man removes it from the wall to take a closer look. Just as he did so, Goodall returns to the office startling him.

"Do you believe in ghosts, kid?" Goodall asks.

"Who is it in the story?" The young man defers.

"Nobody knows kid, but every once in a while a new story turns up about this guy. Some people say he was sent here as a *guardian* to watch over them, others believe that he's only a myth, a legend… Either way, I'd like somebody to explain this." Officer Goodall takes the article from the young mans hands opening it out fully to reveal a photo, albeit a blurry photo.

"This was taken about fifteen years ago by some little Chinese kid." As bad as the photography was, it was easy to make out a large figure seemingly running away from a blazing inferno, with what appeared to be an axe in his hand. The imagery sends a chill up the young mans spine. He finds it quite harrowing.

"What the hell?" He whispers, pausing briefly looking at Goodall with quizzing eyes. Goodall continues.

"Whoever it was pulled three people from the blaze before we got there that night. All the statements from the saved were the same, weird 'eh kid! I remember it like it was yesterday."

Across town, in a basement of a dingy building, Scapatechi and his men are meeting around a large table. All the big shots of organized crime are present. They are engaged in discussing who runs what in the city, as years of turf wars by these men has been the cause of some of the city's most violent fires and deaths. Mostly the innocent suffered as a result. One of the gang lords, Armondo Peratzki, had just served nine years in the pen for second-degree murder. Now back on the streets he wants to take control of newly claimed 'hot areas' and red light districts.

Scapatechi heads the meeting.

"This is how it is… Flynt will continue to run our dirty little hot spots, we think he's been doing a pretty good job while our very own Mr Peratski was banged up, wouldn't you all agree?" With that the meetings humour is directed at a very angry and frustrated Peratski, as they all share in the laughter with Scapatechi. Peratski strongly disagrees, brewing up what could be an extremely dangerous argument. The room falls silent for a few seconds, only broken by the sound of footsteps approaching.

"Flynt," Scapatechi snaps with a cunning smile. Dressed in a well-fitted black suit, a well groomed young man emerges from the shadows.

"Yes sir," says the new face. Flynt was Scapatechi's highly criticised adopted son. He had an extremely unpleasant gift, as a young boy, soon after Scapatechi took him in beneath his wing, it was discovered that the boy was pyrokenetic. He has the ability to produce fire from nowhere, to pro-create flames from his mind, disturbing as it is, Scapatechi loves him for it. Compared to the company present he looks very much refined, kind of 'proper'. Removing his jacket, he reveals a freakish muscle bound physique. He had well designed tattoos covering each arm, and his eyes were extremely dark, almost black. Needless to say the sight of him soon fizzled out any argument that was about to erupt. Peratski backed down, knowing that nobody messes with Scapatechi's adopted son.

"Gentlemen, as I was saying. You control the streets and I control you, it couldn't be anymore simple." Scapatechi whispers in a smooth, calm voice.

The handsome face of Evil

The gang lords are pretty much powerless and visibly frustrated by this show of strength. Peratski found the balls to pipe up once more.

"What about Midtown... Who runs that?" He demands, whist looking towards the other gangsters present for a little support. Midtown has always stayed on the straight and narrow. No corrupt police or injustice, and up to now no gang lord control. It really was the only part of the city that remained pure.

"I'm actually quit glad you asked." Scapatechi responds extremely smug before lighting his cigar. They attending mobsters look on in disbelief as he reveals his plans to them. The plan could be easily described as inhumane. The vision Scapatechi has in mind is in itself disturbing. The madman's aim is to pump oil through the sewers beneath Midtown's streets, giving the citizens enough time to flee he would set it alight, annihilating everything. Somewhere in his crazed twisted mind, he thought with Mid Town in ruins, he would easily seize control and rebuild it as his own dark polluted empire.

Some gang lords present thought Scapatechi was insane, others thought him a genius. The response is pretty mixed, though on the surface they all agreed, well they knew if they did not, they too would be at the end of Scapatechi's fiery pitch fork.

13

Making friendly conversation, a young doctor makes her way through the isles of patients. Nearing the end of the ward she bumps into the head doc of the hospital's paediatrics unit.

"Are you still here girl?" The head doc asks.

"I am Macy, just finishing a few rounds. So much to do and so little time," the woman replies wearily.

"Now get yourself off home, you've been here almost eighteen hours." The head doc tells her in a sympathetic tone.

Without any resistance to the request, the young woman finishes up with her last task then makes her way towards the locker room to get her things together. Soaking her face with cold water, she raises her head and looks at herself in the mirror for a few seconds.

'Wow… You really need a drink girl.' The young woman thinks to herself. Seconds later a few female doctors enter the locker room interrupting the moment.

"Hey, are you still here?" They ask in astonishment.

"Yeah I'm just leaving," she replies before clutching her bag.

Just as she pushes her way through the double doors she overhears one of the female doctors making a sarcastic comment about her being all work and no play, then predictably the locker room erupts with childish giggles.

Passing the reception post, she notices Dr Whiley then suddenly changes her direction; however he manages to catch sight of her from the corner of his eye and swiftly makes direction after her.

Whiley is a stereotype young hotshot Doctor and is notorious for making pretty sleazy, tacky moves on his female colleagues. He is also notorious for getting what he wants, but not with this girl. This one was a challenge to him.

"Hey Rachel, I'm just finishing up in a few minutes if you want to grab a drink somewhere?" Whiley says in a sleazy manor, but trying to be quite the gentleman, though Rachel sees right though his phoney acts, as if it were made from glass.

"Id rather not Dr Whiley, I am a... I am taking my grandmother to watch 'Gone with the Wind' tonight, I am real sorry." Rachel quickly lies before turning on her heels.

"B but!" Whiley stutters. Before he could even get out a single word Rachel was gone like the wind, leaving Whiley standing in the foyer left like a bell boy waiting on a tip.

Making her way, alone, towards her car which is parked on the basement level, she passes one of the hospital outbuildings, and has a sudden uneasy feeling like she is being watched. Keeping her head down, she quickens her pace, knowing the growing rate of muggings, rape and murders in the city and decides not to take any chances. Passing a dark side alley two men lurk in the shadows. She sees them from the corner of her eye but pretends she does not. As she passes the men start to move towards her from behind.

Before they could even exit the alley, a huge wooden handle with a razor sharp piece of steel at the end stops them in their tracks. The terrifying object was none other than a huge customised razor sharp axe. The men were mesmerised at the sudden events that had taken place, as they stood quivering with fear, their terrified eyes followed the thick wooden shaft to find a massive gloved hand grasping tightly on the end of it.

"Bad idea guys," warns the mysterious figure.

In what appeared to be nanoseconds, the blade was pressed firmly beneath the chin of one of the thugs leaving the second to make a run for it, but was soon pinned against the alley wall by the back of the steel axe, leaving him gasping for breath. Struggling and mumbling, the two thugs are lifted straight off the ground by the mysterious hero.

Rachel can only make out the shadows of what's happening. Even that is too much for her imagination, causing her to scream and take off towards the parking lot as fast as her legs would carry her.

The dark phantom now has both men pinned against the wall. He punches a gaping hole next to their heads with his right fist, causing lots of red bricks and dust to beat of the ground as it falls. Pleading for mercy, they paid complete attention when the dark stranger moves in towards them,

"Never try that again… NEVER!" He roars with his face now partly showing, scaring the living hell out of the two low lives. At that moment an unlawful silence falls in the ally as the terrified thugs ran for their pitiful lives. Following them with his eyes, Mason watches them disappear into the darkness.

Once again his mind travels back to his precious daughter.

✳✳✳

"My Daughters in there…" Screamed Mason before punching out the two cops. Now back on his feet Mason scrambled over to the police line and without a second thought he frantically tore it down, leaving the two cops gob smacked. Searching frantically for his little girl, his crew could do nothing but watch on in disbelief as he tried with all his might to tear his way into the bus. Undeterred by the hard twisted metal, he continued, grazing his flesh in his hasty frenzy. Not being able to find her, the anger turned to frustration leading Mason to roar out his daughter's name.

"Lydia…" Interrupting Mason's raging search, Lombardo calmly intervenes.

"She's not in there sir," whispered Lombardo; who he had never met before now.

"She is over here." As Lombardo's words filtered into Masons head, the teary firefighter looked around; there she was lying between two ambulances. Paramedics were treating the precious girl; however Lydia's injuries were internal leaving her without a scratch. Deceptive as her injuries were, she wouldn't make it causing Mason to fall to his knees in front of her, his breaking voice whispered into her ear.

"My brave little girl, you're going to be just fine." The paramedics knew the girl's time was running out; instinctively Mason knew this too causing him to grip his daughter tightly, cradling her back and fro.

***

Suddenly the sirens of a passing squad car startle Mason, once again bringing him from that dark place. As the P.D. squad car draws nearer, Mason makes for home, leaving the squad car search light peering down an empty ally.

"There is nothing down there!" States one of the patrol men while the other shines the search light deep into the alley.

"Lets gets get out of here, this place gives me the creeps," replies the other as he switches off the lamp.

14

Panting and sweating, Tyler hits out at a punch bag; getting rid of all his emotion, all of his anger when suddenly the phone rings. He lets it ring out then finally the answering machine kicks in.

"Hey Tyler, its Debby..."

"Why do you never pick up?"

"Anyway look, you must be busy or something… Babe you know I'd really love to move down there with you but you also know my job means a lot to me, I just don't think New York is for me, please call me."

As Debby hangs up Tyler doesn't show any emotion, he just continues to hammer the punch bag until he can punch no more. With one final blow he sinks his last punch deep into its mid section before turning his eyes to a picture of his family on the wall. He stares at it for a few moments, reminiscing of the good old days, where he suddenly finds himself in his old back yard.

***

"Don't worry boy I'll save you." Tyler assured Rex, though Rex didn't seem scared at all, it was widely whispered that Rex would climb that tree simply to get a break from old Mr Peabody.

"Son, you be careful now, I must go indoors for a few minutes, and your Mom is calling on me!" Mason shouted from across the yard to Tyler.

"Sure Dad no problem, I can handle this job on my own." Young Tyler replied with a brave tone. Lifting his makeshift wooden ladder he and his Dad had made last summer Tyler made his way into Mr Peabody's yard were he propped the ladder at the base of the tree, then started his ascent.

It was only when Tyler was half way up when he noticed that the base of the ladder was rather shaky and looked as if it was going to give way. He had a decision to make, quickly climb back down and ask his Dad to retrieve Rex, or against all odds continue. Deep down in his gut he knew he had to go on.

Just as he had grasped a branch above his right shoulder, the sound of cracking wood startled him, it also startled Rex and with the sound of the buckled ladder Rex lost his footing and got lodged between two branches. Tyler is filled with a real feeling of fear, frantically looking around for his Dad or even old Mr Peabody, but he was alone.

***

When, suddenly a knock at the door startles him. Gathering his thoughts, he says,

"It's open! Come on in."

Not ones to turn down the invite, in barges JJ, Sandy, Kastle and the Torelli brothers.

"Get your ass in gear new guy, its play time." JJ announces. Tyler gives JJ a half smile, grabs his coat and follows his new crew out the door, taking a brief glance at his phone before closing the door; in effect closing the door on Debby.

The Tavern is a typical American bar, both colourful and friendly. It attracts people from all walks of life, from Wall Street stock brokers to side street merchants; it is the place to be on a Friday night. At the far end of the bar a worn out detective sits in a cloud of cigar smoke sipping his Jack Daniels on the rocks.

"Bar tender, fill it up," requests the Detective, sending his empty glass across the bar counter.

"Tough day…" Asks the annoyingly happy barman; this guy has a really smug smile showing a mouth full of pearly whites, there is just something about him, deep down the Detective likes him, but being the guy he is, he doesn't like to show it. The Detective looks straight at him knowing that he is just about to say something else probably annoying when a young lady bursts in startling the barman. Though the tough detective remains focused on him for a few seconds then in his own time he turns on his stool to take a discreet look.

"Oh Rachel, are you alright?" A young lady who was already seated asks the dramatic entrant. After the dramatic events earlier outside the hospital, Rachel had phoned her close friend Sarah asking her to meet in the Tavern.

As Rachel begins to explain the night's happenings to Sarah, she can't help but recall the shadows in the alley, the noises and the screams. She continues the tale as Sarah orders another round of beer.

"That part of the city sure is suffering Rach!" Sarah sighs as she downs the last of her now flat beer.

Just then the door of the Tavern opens, and in walks Tyler with his crew. They make their way straight over to the pool table catching the attention of the cigar smoking Detective as they pass.

"Sure I'll get the first round," Tyler offers.

"You do that new guy!" They all agree. Apparently it was an old tradition for the newest member to get in the first round, well at least that's what they told Tyler. The atmosphere was great in The Tavern; it was welcoming with music, friends and beer, just what Tyler needed?

From the back red bricked wall JJ grabs two pool cues off the rack and stands in front of Tyler.

"Well new guy, can you play?" JJ challenges just before pining his beer. Tyler grabs the cue from JJ.

"Better than u Jack," he counters.

"Hey I told you new guy, my friends call me JJ!" He responds jokingly.

"We'll see bout that," Tyler mutters whilst chalking his cue.

The game gets under way, and manages to attract a rather large crowd. Onlookers are placing bets, and the drinks are flowing, heating the competition further.

Across the bar Rachel, now a little more at ease can't help but notice the commotion at the pool table. Due to the crowd gathering around it, she can't tell who is playing, however every so often she does catch a glimpse of an extremely sexy guy in the middle of it all. Tyler prepares to line up a very crucial shot. He's on the black ball and needs it to win the game but much more than that he needs it to win respect. Knowing the last shot is upon them, the Tavern falls silent as Tyler takes the shot. Messing around, JJ manages to just tip the end of his Tyler's cue, causing the white ball to chip off the table in a dramatic fashion, whistling through the air and just missing the heads of a few onlookers, before ending its journey under a nearby table, resting nicely at the heel of a very attractive young lady.

"God dam it kid! You just cost me fifty bucks," sighs a disappointed gambler. A small crowd remains to watch the rest of the crew play, probably hoping for another exciting match-up. However they can't do much without the flying white ball.

"I think it landed over there somewhere Tyler," cackles one of the Torelli brothers who were by now completely wasted. Tyler heads towards the booths in search for the ball, catching the attention of Rachel who is quite taken by the attractive young stranger.

"Now there's something you don't see every day," mutters Sarah, who instantly opens her compact makeup mirror.

"He's coming over Rach," she excitedly whispers.

"Hmmm, watch and learn girlfriend," Sarah tells Rachel under her breath. Quickly lifting the ball, Sarah shoves it into Rachel's hand waiting eagerly to see if the hot guy will approach them.

A few feet in front of the girls Tyler gets down on his hands and knees looking under the tables for the white ball, when a soft voice offers,

"Looking for this?" Hearing the voice Tyler sharply jolts up banging his head off the table, Rachel's eyes light up when she finally gets his attention. He is by now totally embarrassed, especially when he realises how beautiful she is.

"Ah, wow, shit, sorry about that, I mean the ball, Oh and the cue…ah…" An embarrassing flustered Tyler stutters. He looks back towards the guys, as if looking for a bit of support, and catches JJ pointing over and laughing.

'What an idiot....' Tyler thinks to himself.

"It's fine, honestly!" Rachel smiles; trying her best to pull him in.

"He's hot!" Sarah whispers from beneath a cough, but before any conversation could even begin, Dr Whiley from the Hospital steps in, putting Rachel completely on the spot.

"Hey Rachel aren't you going to introduce me?" He asks with a very pretend look of excitement on his face.

"Ahhh, this is…" Rachel stumbles as she realises she actually doesn't even know the guys name. Noticing the situation Tyler quickly answers for Rachel.

"The name's Tyler, Tyler Hope." Tyler butts in, reaching out his hand as he speaks. Whiley can't help but grind his teeth at Tyler's confidence; however he does manage a forceful handshake.

"I'm a firefighter down on 52nd," he continues. He may have been shaking Dr Whiley's hand, but he was staring right at Rachel the whole time, as if in a trance. Thing was, Rachel was returning the favour.

"Am I interrupting something?" Dr Whiley sarcastically asks noticing their flirtatious looks. The presence of Dr Whiley definitely put a damper on the mood. I thankfully interrupted this awkward moment comes a yell from Sandy.

"We really got to roll Tyler, we got training tomorrow, remember?" She snaps basically showing her control over the guys for the benefit of the two women. The crew who were just getting in the mood get ready to leave,

"God damn it, where the hell does the time go?" JJ complains, who had just latched his eyes on to Rachel's friend Sarah. Though Tyler had heard their call, he seems unresponsive and wasn't really paying much attention as his eyes are fixed on Rachel's. However, this didn't go unnoticed by Whiley, who quickly snaps.

"Does anyone want a drink?"

"I'm buying!" As if he was trying to buy their company.

"No thanks' maybe another time," smirks Tyler, suddenly coming out of his trance with Rachel.

"Ok, some other time," mimics Whiley; It was certainly plain to see that the two men had got off on the wrong foot.

"Lets hit the bar guys," Whiley sneers to his friends. As they stand at the counter he turns to his snobbish friends and asks what they want to drink. Before they even had a chance to reply, Whiley is met with a visibly angry Sarah.

"You're a real jerk Whiley!" With that, Sarah lifts a near by glass of corona catching him completely off guard she unhesitant throws it in his face. Sarah's gesture gets a reaction from most of the bar. Cheers and whistles, especially from the women erupted The Tavern sending Whiley into a furious embarrassing flurry. Sarah storms out grabbing Rachel and Tyler on her way. The discreet detective, shrouded in smoke follows.

15

As a large 36oz steak cooks on the frying pan, a faint song on the radio can just be heard through the crackle of the sparking fat...

'Love is a burning thing, and it makes a fiery ring, bound by wild desire, I fell into a ring of fire.' The chef prepares and tosses a salad before setting the table as he sings along to the words.

"Something sure does smell good," calls an extremely hungry voice. The chef turns to greet the visitor.

"Sure does Dale! Did you get the beer alright, friend?"

"Yeah Mason, ice cold and extra large of course." Dale, now much older stands in the doorway with a huge grin on his face. The men have become accustomed to the lifestyle they had chosen to live, huge steaks cold beer, not forgetting saving the occasional life from time to time. The two men talk for a while about how the steak should be cooked. Dale always wants a well-done steak, but, in typical fashion Mason enjoys it rare. This was always an issue on 'steak night' as they only had one frying pan, but at the end of the discussion the two would usually settle for medium. On this occasion though, Dale tries to keep the discussion going for that little bit longer; the way Dale figures, the longer it cooks the better it is for him.

Mason is still impressively huge; although years of fighting his way through infernos had begun to take their toll. He is showing signs of wear and tear, but was by no means finished.

"How long are we going to keep doing this for Mason?" Dale asks, out of the blue.

"What, steak night? As long as there are cows Dale," laughs Mason. Dale smiles, but doesn't laugh.

"No I mean all this, everything…" There's a meaningful silence. Mason stops and thinks about Dale's words for a few seconds then finally answers.

"For as long as Scapatechi and his gang keep burning and destroying our city, I'll be here fighting and that's for how long!" The huge firefighter finishes off his steak in silence, still angered at the thought of the Scapatechi crew continuing their terror campaign, he lifts his plate and walks towards the lounge area' dropping his plate in the sink as he passes.

With a roaring open fire to warm them, Mason stokes it with a poker. He just sits down when Dale enters the lounge.

"Look Mason, I know you need to be alone right now, but before I go know this, you're not alone, we will fight these dirt bags until the end." Dale's emotional words hit Mason in the gut, causing him to mellow out a bit.

"I will be down in the work shop if you need me big guy." Dale mutters.

"Ok Dale, one other thing just before you go, steak doesn't taste that bad when cooked well done." Mason says with a half smile.

"Maybe next time…" Dale laughs before turning towards the workshop.

A few blocks from the Tavern, Rachel Sarah and Tyler stands on a sidewalk trying to flag down a cab. Spits of rain start to fall from the sky, gradually picking up speed soaking them through to the skin.

"Here, allow me." Tyler implies remembering his manors. He takes of his light brown suede jacket and places it around Rachel's shoulders sheltering her from the elements, leaving him wearing no more than a white muscle vest. Rachel says nothing at first; she just looks at him with puppy eyes before whispering.

"Oh, thank you," biting her lower lip as she whispers. Sarah notices the blossoming fairy tale romance as she stands in the rain.

"Oh please, get me a bucket!" She echoes across to them just as a passing car whizzes past her pumping its horn, though deep down she longed for that kind of affection.

"You sure have some unusual friends Tyler." Rachel says while pulling the suede jacket even tighter around her shoulders.

"Yeah, there ok I guess." Tyler responds while looking at Rachel as much to say '*look who's talking*' judging by Sarah's antics in the bar a while ago. Just then a yellow cab spots Sarah and makes a hasty u-turn on the near empty road. The cab screeches up along side the trio and stops abruptly causing Sarah to jump back a few steps.

"Watch were you're driving that heap of junk, huh!" Sarah shouts at the Egyptian cab driver, who now looks pretty worried.

"No English?" The cabby responds in a regretful tone.

"Yeah, never worry about it cabby, just turn this piece of junk around and take me and my girl here up town… Can you manage that?" Sarah demands as she jumps into the back seat before squeezing the rain water from her hair.

"Well, I guess this is me…" Rachel says while trying to ignore Sarah's embarrassing behaviour.

"I guess it is Rachel." Tyler replies before walking her to the door of the cab. Before getting in Rachel turns to Tyler and thanks him once more for the jacket and the company.

"Here you'll need this." Rachel offers while taking off the suede jacket.

"No, you hold on to it, you might need it if this cabby drops you off a block or two from your place, lets face it, the way things are going in there, its possible." Tyler replies whilst turning his attention to Sarah and the Egyptian cabby who are by now bickering like cat and dog.

"You could be right about that Tyler." Rachel says while giving Sarah a look of horror.

"Don't worry about her; Sarah and alcohol are not the best combination." Rachel laughs as he climbs into the cab. Tyler can't help but notice how sexy Rachel looks with his jacket wrapped around her and her wet jeans which are now much more hip hugging than before due to the rain.

As the cabby drives off Rachel turns her head and looks out the back window at Tyler, she also can't help but notice how hot he is standing there on the sidewalk with the rain water trickling down his well toned shoulders following the definitive muscular track down his arms. The two continue to lock eyes until the cab hangs a hard left to avoid an oncoming Pepsi truck.

'Jesus, that was pretty close…' Tyler thinks to himself whilst biting his fist.

As he prepares to make way for home a distant cars headlamps light up causing him to shield his eyes from the beam.

"What the…" Tyler questions to himself before taking a few steps back. The mystery driver rolls past him though Tyler can't get a good look at him as a trail of cigar smoke hides the stranger's identity. As the car drives off into the night Tyler feels a shiver race up his spine.

16

Though older, Scapatechi is still equally as ruthless as he always was. The notorious mobster sits at the head of a long mahogany table which is situated in the centre of a very dark room. The room holds a warm orange glow, showing the faces of all present, apart from Scapatechi himself whose face remains in darkness.

"I trust the Midtown plan is in motion?" He asks before delving into his jacket pocket for a cigar. The eeriness of his silhouette is felt through out the room; all present knows that Scapatechi is a man who likes simple yes or no answers and won't accept, cant or wont. He likes to keep things simple. If he doesn't get the answer he wants, well let's just say, he lets his Tommy gun do the talking.

"Y-Y-Yes boss, our best men are working on it as we speak," stammers a petrified goon. Waiting for Scapatechi's response, a bead of sweat sits on the goon's forehead like a drop of rain upon a leaf. To his relief Scapatechi replies,

"Excellent," he states in an unnerving psychotic tone. Turning in his chair towards the roaring open fire, he lights up his cigar, the flames of which reveal his evil face sending shivers up the goon's spine.

Lurking in the shadows, a team of goons make their way beneath the midtown streets to prepare for the twisted events that will soon be motioned. Their leader is none other than the chillingly evil Flynt, who by now due to his status with the boss is a high ranker in the organisation, with unlimited access to vast amounts of drugs, guns and sex. His persona is understandably charismatic as he has it all, although it was widely whispered that his dark desires for feisty young call girls was as sinister as it was fatal, for the call girls of course.

"Ok boy's, you know what you have got to do, so get your asses in gear and do it!" Flynt demands as he stands high over them. At his request the goons start to descend with bundles of piping and other necessary materials for the job. Knowing they can't afford to be seen in the area Flynt orders the goons to move discreetly as a tight unit. Within minutes, a few of the goons formed welding teams and start to connect large piping together piece-by-piece, directing it deep into midtowns under ground. The heavy workload was intense though Flynt continues to push the goons to their limit as he knew he could not fail Scapatechi.

Standing in the centre of a makeshift steel platform Flynt's eyes are caught by welding sparks which seem to light up the underground, some how twigging a distant memory.

***

The rain seemed to last for days, even weeks Michael recalled. His parents were out though were soon to be home, collecting Rachel from Mrs Garbonee on their way, but time seemed to stand still for him. Waiting there alone listening to the constant batter of rain clatter off the windows was a living nightmare, causing him to sit on the bare planked floor with his hands over his ears praying for the rain to stop. Then to his surprise as if from nowhere, a sudden bolt of lightening lit up the night sky out side, soon to follow was the monstrous roar of thunder which echoed throughout the docks causing him to jump with sheer shock. Once more he closed his eyes and prayed not to be alone any more. Seconds later a second crack of lightening struck down, though this time if felt closer, when suddenly every bulb in the dingy apartment seemed to glow brighter than ever. The bulbs made a low humming sound which gradually grew higher in pitch, until they did what Michael had sensed they would do. As if planed, every bulb in the apartment seemed to blow at once causing bursts of sparks to shroud over him, each one like a needle to his skin. Soon the apartment was in darkness and Michael lay cradled on the ground rubbing his arms were the sparks had rested. He continued to lie on the cold floor, in the darkness as the second roar of monstrous thunder made its way through the apartment. Hey lay in Darkness, he lay in pain, he lay alone.

∗∗∗

Eventually completing the pipe work, the order is given.

"Ok, let it go!" Flynt roars with a firm tone of authority. Word is passed to each gang member, eventually reaching the surface, giving the guy at the end the signal to unleash the oil. With a horrendous scratching sound he turns the huge valve that's feeding off local gas stations and parked tanker trucks, which were hijacked, from out of town. Scapatechi's insane plan springs into action.

At the firehouse, the crew seem to be taking well to their new team-mate. The atmosphere is professional and friendly, with Ding and Kastle now cleaning the engines.

"Hey, come on man, save the water for the engine!" Ding shouts whilst cracking a smile, when Kastle empties a bucket of water over him.

"You two idiots!" Sandy sounds from underneath the engine.

"Knock it off you two." Goodall barks before Kastle directs the attention over to Tyler,

"Hey Tyler… You picked a hell of a time to start here!" Kastle shouts as he dries him self off.

"Sure new guy! Maybe you should have started like next month." One of the Torelli brothers adds jokingly.

"Leave him alone guys, I think he's got what it takes," countered the other.

"What would that be?" Tyler asks in a defensive tone. Breaking up the hacking match, Goodall interrupts.

"Ok, gather round and listen to me!" Goodall yells so loud that the hard of hearing would have been fine.

"Today of course is the day you've all been looking forward to Gentlemen, its training day!" His last sentence initiated a huge grin from ear to ear. Goodall always loved training day, maybe because he got a soft seat, a whistle and a mug of black coffee. His aim was to push the crew to their physical and mental limits. A fair trade Goodall thought.

Goodall was one tough cookie. With his stone cold look you could just tell he certainly worked hard for those medals of his.

"Ok people listen up, you know the drill, oh and Tyler… Just you try and keep up, ok?" Tyler took one look at Goodall, and with a half smile he responds,

"Piece of cake," as he eyeballs the record times on the board.

The training was tough, they all knew it, though to Goodall's surprise Tyler was certainly no slow coach either. Hours past like minutes and it seems like no time when JJ was shouting over to Tyler,

"Had enough yet?" Only the two of them were left in the circuit running as the others could take no more.

"Just warming up JJ, how about you?" Tyler responds who is by now frantically panting for breath. The two ran side by side nudging each other, trying to out do each other like two competitive school boys.

"Let's just call it a tie this time," JJ offers, his legs now feeling like two rubber pipes.

"Now that was intense Guys." Sandy says in flirtatious tones. She was now all hot and sweaty and running off towards the hanger when she turns her head towards Kastle and the Torelli brothers who were following her quite closely. Not taking Sandy's saucy bait Tyler and JJ ease back from the rest and continue lifting the training gear from the yard.

"So, what's your story Tyler?" JJ asks curiously whilst throwing a towel over his right shoulder.

"Well it's the usual story bud, my dad was a firefighter and his dad, and you know how it goes."

Tyler answers, much easier than he would have done before. JJ lifts the hose to his shoulder and stumbles a little,

"Wow, let me!" Tyler comes straight over to help. This didn't go unnoticed, as JJ spares Tyler a nod of thanks.

"So, is your old man still active?" JJ continues.

"No, ah, he died along time ago." Tyler says outright.

"I'm sorry Tyler, was it in the line of duty?" JJ asks, trying not to sound nosy.

"Yeah, he died in the September Dockland fire, as I said, it was long time ago." A respectful silence falls between the men. Then suddenly it dawns on JJ...

"Holy shit, your Dad was a Blue Angel!" He blurts out with excitement.

"I mean, sorry to hear man, its just they're legendary, some people actually believe that one the *fallen angels* still shows his face from time to time," an extremely excited JJ rants. With that, Tyler looks upon JJ with a feeling of emotional eruption; a mixture of hope, anger, excitement and sorrow. As his mind flashes back to the newspaper cutting on Goodall's wall he starts fitting the pieces together.

However his concentration is broken by a sweet 'hi' from a surprising guest who has just appeared at the station door holding what appears to be a dry cleaned suede jacket under her arm. Her presence takes Tyler by complete surprise.

'Damn, she's beautiful', he thinks to himself. Not knowing where to look, he grabs one of the cleaning cloths from Ding to clean himself up a bit as he is covered in sweat and oil leaving his vest stuck to his body. He wouldn't have been so self-conscious if he knew that Rachel actually found it quite attractive.

"Ahh, I was wondering if I could have a word with you." Rachel asks feeling quite embarrassed, as everyone had stopped what they were doing and turned round to look at her.

Showing just a little more confidence than last time, Tyler takes a few steps towards Rachel and greets her half way. Before they engage in conversation Rachel hands over the jacket to Tyler causing the crew to watch on in anticipation.

"Look ah… I don't normally do this." Rachel says to Tyler while trying to ignore Sandy's stern stare. Noticing the friction between the two women, Tyler swiftly moves him self between them blocking each other from view.

"Ah... I better go." Rachel whispers in a shy and timid voice.

"No, wait a minute Rach, you just got down here, it wouldn't be very mannerly of me to send you away like this, now would it?" Tyler replies while placing the jacket on a nearby hanger before ushering her towards a spare fire truck.

"You guys don't mind do you?" He cheekily asks.

"You've got ten minutes Tyler!" Goodall answers, not realising how it sounded at the time.

"Certainly a livewire that one," Goodall mutters under his breath.

"Oh my God, I cannot believe you just did that Tyler!" Rachel chastises who by now is totally embarrassed.

"Don't you worry about it; those guys think that you're as crazy as I am." Tyler laughs before throwing her a wink.

"Shall we go for a drive then?" He suggests to Rachel who has a very worried look in her eyes.

"I don't know Tyler, is it safe?" She quizzes.

"I only came down to apologise for the other night," she tells him. With that, Tyler put his fire truck in gear and makes his way down town, with the lights and sirens flashing traffic just opened up for them.

"This is great, isn't it Rach? Oh, what were you saying there! That guy," laughs Tyler.

"You don't have to apologise for that guy, what was his name again?" Tyler offers.

"Whiley," Rachel responds while gripping tightly to her seat.

"Yeah, Whiley," Tyler concurs.

"I do actually, he's such a jerk, and he works with me," Rachel continues with a sigh.

"Oh let me guess… You're an innocent little nurse and old Whiley was lucky enough to steal a kiss from you at the Christmas party and every since he still thinks he owns you." Tyler answers smugly.

"Impressive Tyler, close but yet so far away! I'm a doctor, burns specialist actually, and no, Dr Whiley did not steal a kiss at the Christmas party. That would be nasty!" Rachel chuckles; now quite relaxed as she's risen above her embarrassment.

Rachel pretends not to notice Tyler's well-toned muscular arms, which just happened to be covered in sweat. Without any more words, they both feel the chemistry between themselves. After circling the city for a while Rachel decides that she wants to return to the station.

"Aren't you worried about your boss, what's his name…?" Rachel asks, pausing briefly.

"Goodall," Tyler adds.

"Old Goodall's bark is worse than his bite Rach." Tyler says to Rachel with a confident smile.

"You really are an original, you know that!"

"Why thanks Rach, I better be careful not to loose my newly acquired status then."

Now pulling back up to the hanger in his station, Rachel flirtatiously turns her head while trying to get out of the fire truck but being the girly girl she is, she cannot. Tyler jumps out of the engine and the crew all try to look busy. The reality is they love gossip of course. He goes round to Rachel's side to help her down. She stumbles from the door, and he catches her.

"What's with this girl?" Sandy expresses as she rolls her eyes. The others just laugh to themselves. Tyler walks Rachel to the door, where their eyes meet. Rachel can't help but think how familiar they are. She decides not to mention this, well not yet anyway.

"Look hot shot, I'm not the kind of girl that needs saving. I could have got down from there if you'd given me a chance!" She says in a faux defensive tone.

"Oh yeah, well I bet you a kiss that I will have to save you sometime, so until that time your lips are yours," Tyler ventures.

"Even if you do have to save me, which I doubt very much, who says you will get a chance to kiss them?" Rachel teases in reply. She drives off, leaving a very elated Tyler punching the air,

"He shoots, he scores..." He shouts to the guys with confidence. His winning feeling is soon deflated when Sandy throws an oil covered rag towards him hitting him on the chest; this action got a bigger cheer from the crew though it causes a mutual dry atmosphere between Tyler and Sandy undeterred by the others.

17

From the shadows, a voice calls,

"Mason. Over here!" The voice belongs to Detective Frank Lombardo; the mysterious guy in the Tavern with the cigar. Mason steps towards Lombardo, but both remain in the shadows of a back alley, hidden from view.

"Mason, we got some information on Scapatechi's movements." Mason looks on in anticipation.

"Internal sources claim he's going to take Midtown! We're not sure how yet but we're working on it!" Mason pushes out his massive chest as he takes a deep breath.

"What about your guys?" He asks.

"Mason, you know the department is stretched to the limit. We just have not got the man power, plus he's got most of our guys in his pocket," pleads the Detective.

"That guy shouldn't be breathing Lombardo!"

"Look around you, look at this city! It's his work. His evil that is eating through it, look at what that bastard did to me, I've been battling him for years." Lombardo bows is head before giving Mason an understanding look.

"I'm tired Frank!" Mason sighs in an uncharacteristically emotional tone.

"Look Mason, I've known you a long time now. I've kept your secret. You will have to trust me on this. If we take him this time, I promise you this, he won't breathe again," Lombardo passionately counters.

After the Dockland accident Lombardo followed his instincts of what he had seen and heard in the shadows near Mason's home, he managed to track the phantom firefighter down. Only then did he discover that the ghostly figure he had witnessed was Mason, the man he had met on that tragic morning of the bus crash. From that moment, Lombardo, Dale and Mason made a pact; a ring of trust was formed between the men. Understanding that the powers granted would be used for pure justice, it would be a combined team of the Police Department's knowledge and trust and Fire Department's courage and strength that would effectively serve the city of New York with honour.

Lombardo and Mason

"I take it you could use the Fire Department on this one, eh," Jokes Mason in his deep, rough voice. As the firefighter turns to the shadows ready to take off Lombardo echoes after him,

"Ah, one more thing Mason," Lombardo calls. Mason stops in his tracks and turns to Lombardo,

"Yeah, what is it Frank?" He queries.

"Well remember the other night when you told me about Rachel's ordeal? I came across her down in the Tavern and Mason you wouldn't believe who walked in." There is an uneasy silence as Mason impatiently waits for Lombardo's next words.

"It's your boy, Tyler, he's back and he has fulfilled his childhood dream Mason."

Love, pain, and loneliness suddenly races through Mason's blood stream. It's all flooding back to him but he doesn't show any emotion.

Instead he turns and makes off into the darkness once more,

"My boy…" He whispers.

Two solid doors of Scapatechi's office creaks open, casting the shadow of a man onto the room floor.

"You wanted to see me?" The visitor asks anxiously.

"Yes Peratski, come in, come in, have a drink," Scapatechi offers with a cunning smile. All the city's crime lords are again present, looking on anxiously at the unimaginable drama that is about to take place. Peratski, looking more and more nervous as Scapatechi wasn't normally this nice, so he downs the glass of scotch in one gulp. Peratski has a feeling deep down in his gut that something isn't right.

"I understand that your feelings on the Midtown operation are questionable Peratski?" Scapatechi directs in a bittersweet tone.

It was well known among his peers that Peratski always hated the ground that Scapatechi walked on; he also strongly disagrees with the fact that he would have full control of New York and he thought his Midtown plans were completely insane.

"Well I think your methods are a little questionable." Peratski flatly offers.

"Well need I remind you, I have access to every contact of terror in this city?" Scapatechi states proudly. A visibly nervous Peratski snaps,

"Look, I want out!" A very uncomfortable silence ensues.

"There's only one way out Peratski." Without delay, Flynt appears behind Scapatechi. Peratski's body becomes limp and lifeless. He clutches at his throat with both hands and tries to shout.

"You bastard, you poisoned me." An evil Scapatechi has a twisted satisfied look on his face when answering,

"Yes, yes I did, though I didn't think that you would finish off the scotch so fast," he says with a very fake laugh.

"Oh and one other thing Peratski, did you think I wouldn't find out about your little meetings with the P.D. you idiot, I own this town remember!" Scapatechi shouts as he slams down his glass.

Still conscious, Peratski feels his now dying body being dragged off towards a warm glowing light; unaware that Flynt was dragging him towards the roaring open fire.

"ARRRRRRGGGHHHH!" Peratski screams as a heartless Flynt and another goon toss him into the fire.

"May that be a warning to anyone who thinks it's wise to have a personal relationship with any personnel from our pathetic police force?" Scapatechi informs the room. The men around the table look like they are going to throw up. Without any more prompting, they all agree with Scapatechi 100%, hell, possibly even 110%. With all eyes firmly on a sadistic Scapatechi, these guys know that things are getting out of control; I mean how far can one crazy mobster go? Now turning to his Son he calmly orders,

"My boy, visit Peratski's den down in hells kitchen. Break the sad news to his goons, their ultimatum is this, to join us and have it all, if not they can share a similar fate as their now very retired boss.

"It's up to them, Good boy."

"Yes father," Flynt replies with a chilling look from his soulless eyes.

18

A fiery hotspot named 'Little Vegas' parties into the night. The oblivious attendees have no idea that Scapatechi's henchmen are growing ever closer to their hidden pleasures. The club was alive with black jack tables and roulette wheels, surrounded with isles upon isles of silver dollar slot machines. The place is a dream come true for any corrupt cop or politician that wants a taste of the city's forbidden fruits.

Unknown to the punters, that the owner, the late Mr Peratski had just been poisoned then burned alive! In the main lounge corrupt police officers openly parade around with their uniforms still on with their top three buttons removed obviously. They have drunk and drugged hookers on each arm, stopping from time to time to talk with pimps and dealers along the way. Within the dark establishment hidden booths hold wealthy businessmen and mobsters' a-like enjoying sleazy lap dances from scantily clad young foreign women; it is a true den of iniquity. Security is tight down here as Peratski's men guard every door.

Pulling up about twenty yards away from the club, the team of goons get out and make their way across to a near by alley.

"Stay here!" Flynt hisses. He has a plan. Covering his face with the lapels of his jacket, Flynt makes his way around to the side door. He approaches the doorman pretending to be a drunk. While his gang look on from a near by alley he continues the charade.

"Get out of here, you drunken loser!" One of the doormen retorts. However, upon closer inspection, his suspicions are aroused; catching the glare of the drunk's eye the doorman senses a familiar instinct.

"Wait a minute! Don't I know y…y…you?" The other doorman questions, but before he has time to finish his sentence, Flynt has a nine millimetre pistol pressing against his forehead.

"Your boss is dead. The way I see it you've got one choice," Flynt bluntly states.

"We will never join Scapatechi, he's insane! Anyway we have our own world down here!" The doorman stutters.

There is a sudden bang and a spray of brain, blood and skull hit the back wall, sending the doorman to the ground with a heavy thud.

"Wrong answer," echoes Flynt in a heartless tone. Now turning to the other doorman, who was now shaking in his boots, Flynt drops his arm resting the pistol at his side.

"Thank you, thank you!" Praises the frightened doorman for not shooting him too; however Flynt had another agenda for this one. With his pyrokenetic abilities Flynt turns his back on the doorman and starts walking off towards his gang, as he does the guard spontaneously burst into flames. Screaming wildly with the pain of burning alive the doorman drops to his knees in agonising pain before his incinerated carcass falls forward onto the sidewalk. As Flynt walks away he whispers to himself,

"Maybe you would have preferred a bullet?" He asks with an evil grin on his face.

The gang quickly infiltrate the building, making their way to the maintenance access corridors. There they plant explosives throughout the lower levels. Peratski's Little Vegas will soon be coming to an end, just as a Peratski himself had. As they set the devices through out the lower level one of the goons looks confused.

"Shit, where are the detonators?" He shouts with a look of determination.

"Do not worries about those, just you guys get your asses out of here?" Orders Flynt as he sets the final bomb. As the goons make their way out, Flynt slowly walks down the long access corridor where they had just planted the bombs. His expression becomes completely lifeless as he delves deep into his mind harnessing his abilities. Passing through the eerie dark corridor he is able to detonate each device by sending ferocious amounts of energy into the explosives causing them to blow.

Watching on from a distance at the wild explosions the goons thought that Flynt was surely dead, however to their disbelief they look on in astonishment when he appears from the smouldering glow undeterred by the ferocious flames.

On the upper levels of Little Vegas the crowd burst into wild hysteria after hearing the explosions. Cops pull their zips up and reach in for their six shooters; pimps grab their hookers, making sure they don't get away, though not before the hookers quickly snatch as much drugs and money as they possibly can before everyone frantically staggers towards the fire exits.

19

Now back at the Fire House the guys have just returned from a domestic fire call out.

"That old lady sure was lucky!" JJ exclaims with a hint of sincerity.

"Apparently she fell asleep as she waited for dinner to cook." Ding jokes as he shakes his head in disbelief.

"Ha... ha... It could have been worse Ding, it could have been your cooking," laughs Sandy. Just as one of the Torelli brothers was about to make another wisecrack about old peoples cooking, the alarm bells sound. They all look at each other with a real grim expression before Tyler says what everyone was thinking,

"Here we go again!"

The fire house doors fly open and the engine spins out to the main street with blue flashing lights and sirens blazing. The roaring engine hastily makes its way towards Hell's Kitchen.

Across town, the towering firefighter stands tall on the rooftop of the old station. Looking across the city he can't help but think of his precious family, his lost daughter and now the return of his boy. Lombardo's words seem to echo through his mind like a beating drum. The return of his Son pulls him mind in so many different directions.

Inside the Station the red warning beckons begin to flash. Dale quickly makes his way up to the roof top to notify Mason of the emergency, but to Dales surprise Mason has already gone. Dale walks to the edge of the roof top and can just make out Mason's silhouette darting towards Hell's kitchen.

"God speed my friend," he whispers to himself as he watches Mason disappear beneath the shadow of night.

Mason leaps from rooftop to rooftop, his fire jacket blows in the wind like the sail of an old ghost ship sailing from the abyss. He battles his way towards the danger that lies ahead by using his axe to pull him onto high ledges and to smash his way through any obstacles that gets in his way. As he approaches the flaming building he leaps to a lower roof were he notices on the streets below a fire crew 'equally dedicated as he' pulling up to the blazing building.

A shadowy figure darts past the engine, quickly penetrating a side window. The sound of smashing glass catches the attention of the fire crew as they step out of the truck.

"What the hell was that?" Sandy expresses with a shock fuelled gasp.

"The window was broken from outside, as if something smashed it's way in," Tyler adds whilst kneeling down before picking up a shard of glass. However, as the fire tears on they can't help but hear the screams from the people trapped inside turning their attention to the problem at hand; though Tyler keeps Sandy's words in mind as he prepares his crew for entry.

"JJ, you and I will lead,"

"Scout out the entire building, the rest of you guys can try to control the blaze from out here!" Tyler shouts above the roaring flames. Sandy quickly unrolls the hose before Kastle, Ding and the Torelli brothers start connecting it together leaving Goodall to hook it up to the hydrant.

"Take you're positions guys and lets go," comes a shout from Tyler.

Working as a controlled team to fight this ferocious blaze, their first priority is to save who ever they can, then get out alive. On their way in JJ is met with screaming victims as they run for safety nearly knocking him to the ground.

"Are you alright JJ?" Tyler asks before ushering the screaming people to the paramedics.

By now more ambulance crews arrive and start attending to those who got out first leaving JJ and Tyler to continue their way though towards the ground floor. Scouting every room and booth they can find, they continue fighting their way through the fire, eventually finding themselves at the foot of a grand staircase.

"JJ, I'll go up first you follow, stay close!" Tyler commands.

"Sure Tyler." JJ replies with grit determination.

The brave young firefighters make their way up the stairs, which open up to a large dance floor. It is hard for them to see any movement due to the thick black smoke.

"Over here Tyler, I think I've found something!" JJ yells from behind one of the booths. He has found two victims, unconscious due to smoke inhalation.

"Can you manage, JJ?" Tyler asks conscious of the possibility that there could be others in need of help. JJ looks at Tyler with an assuring look.

"Yeah, just be careful, ok, we don't want to loose you already."

With one man over his left shoulder and another under his right arm JJ battles his way down the stairs towards the side door. Knowing time is against him and more so against the victims he is carrying, he stays strong and makes his way towards the exit.

Tyler carefully manoeuvres his way to the end of the dance floor when he suddenly hears a cry for help. Calculating his every move, he knows that one misjudgement could be fatal; he follows the cries down a smoke-filled corridor. The flames are quickly climbing from below leaving Tyler with only moments to spear. Somewhere through the thick blanket of smoke he can just make out the figure of a girl curled up on the floor.

"Hold on, I'm coming over!" Tyler shouts before making a hasty dash in her direction. As he nears closer he notices a deep void in the floor separating her from him.

"Hold on, I'm coming over!" Tyler assures the girl who is now hysterical with fear."

"Please… Help me!" She splutters.

"Damn it, There's no way around!" Tyler chants to himself. His only option is to back track round to another corridor, which runs parallel to this one.

"Please, stay calm… I *will* save you!" Tyler promises the girl. Turning around Tyler begins to panic as he feels the heat on his face, however just before he gives up hope; he notices another firefighter coming towards him.

"JJ, is that you," roars a puzzled Tyler. Through the smoke Tyler soon notices that this mysterious firefighter is not JJ, nor any of his team. The huge figure was galloping towards him at a tremendous speed, unsure of whom or what this guy is Tyler leaps aside to let the harrowing figure pass. Their eyes meet briefly at their passing causing Tyler's instincts and emotions to merge together at once, his gut churns, and his head feels light. A second later Tyler lifts his head and mutters the words,

"It's you…" He stands in total disbelief when his mind casts itself back to the old newspaper article on Goodall's wall; he envisions the old article picture in his mind, over and over again.

The sheer sight of this huge firefighter stuns Tyler. With his heart pulsating at a great rate he can do nothing but watch as the mysterious figure leaps over the burning void, sweeping the girl up in his arms before pulverising the heavy block wall behind her; creating a whole new meaning to the term emergency exit. With the erotic dancer girl safely in his arms Mason jumps right through the gaping whole landing on the ground below, with a heavy thud he leaves a small impact crater. Kneeling for a second to get his bearings, he pats the dust from his shoulders. Onlookers are open-mouthed with amazement when the huge smoking firefighter lays the young lap dancer on the sidewalk for the ambulance crew to attend. Suddenly he has an instinct, then glances up where he notices Flynt and the gang sitting suspiciously in a van looking on as their handy work embroils. Flynt notices the huge firefighter and within seconds he puts his van in gear and speeds off leaving two tracks of burning rubber, closely followed by Mason in hot pursuit.

"Who the hell was that guy?" Tyler yells; his voice laced with confusion as he makes his way from the building. No one could answer him.

Chasing the beat-out white van down the busy streets of New York, Mason uses the high buildings to his advantage. Leaping from rooftop to rooftop his Birdseye view watches eagerly as the van takes a series of turns down side streets and back alleys; though Mason soon closes in as he knows every side street and short cut like the back of his hand. Through the steaming streets Mason manages to latch on to the back doors of the van, hanging on for a few seconds before using his great strength to break the latch. However before he can do anything else, the doors are forcefully kicked open by one of the goons, knocking Mason to the street in a fast and furious momentum. Hitting the breaks, the van swerves to a screeching stop ending up tight against graffiti sprayed walls, silence follows.

As Mason comes to, he staggers to his feet, but when he gets there he is met with a strong fist to his large square jaw, sending him hurling into a nearby dumpster.

"Not so tough now Mr Fire man," cackles one of the on looking senseless goons.

"Shut your mouth," snaps Flynt.

"This is between me and the big guy!"

But before Flynt could even say another word Mason smashes his huge fist into the side of Flynt's head sending him across the alley into a red brick wall; *I mean that's got to hurt!*

"Why are you doing this Michael?" Mason hesitantly asks. A murmur from Flynt's busted mouth sounds,

"My name is Flynt, not Michael."

"Michael died along time ago." At that moment the terrified goons quickly scamper off into the darkness, leaving the two men alone in the alley with only the light from the beat out van's head lamps to illuminate their battle ground.

Mason slowly walks over to the beaten down bad guy, though to Mason's surprise Flynt suddenly jolts up with full power, sending the two powerful beings into full attack.

The two continue to battle furiously, their beatings echoing through out the alley causing tenants of nearby apartment blocks to open their windows and hang out to watch the monstrous brawl. Frustration starts eating at Flynt as he now starts to feel Mason's wrath, the fact of not winning this fight becomes apparent forcing him to uses his pyrokenetic powers on Mason. However due to Mason's condition he is totally immune to Flynt's dirty tricks and continues the battering. Grabbing Flynt by the throat Mason throws him towards the van sending Flynt hurdling into the side panel with a heavy thud. Getting over powered by Mason, Flynt closes his eyes and concentrates deeply. Within seconds the alley starts to shake, Mason can feel the slight vibrations trembling up through his boots before the van explodes bursting into flames. This catches Mason completely off guard and the useful decoy gives Flynt the chance to scarper off to lick his wounds. Mason stands on and peers into the flames for a few seconds before he himself fades into the darkness.

20

Already flooded with patients, the pressure heightens with the fire down in Hell's Kitchen.

"How many more are there?" Rachel asks her voice weary.

"Not sure Rachel, quite a lot I think!" The staff nurse replies. Rachel who is now completely rushed off her feet blows her hair from her face and grabs two medical charts from the basket. Totally absorbed in the pandemonium, a sudden thump catches Rachel's attention, to her surprise it is the double doors of the room being kicked open, even more surprisingly it is Tyler carrying a very provocative lap dancer in his arms that just happens to be wrapped in his firefighter jacket. At first Rachel's emotions are mixed. They are an unhealthy combination of stress, anger, excitement and even jealousy. However Rachel soon comes to her senses putting away feelings of schoolgirl jealousy orders Tyler to leave the girl on the end bed.

"Why are you here?" She asks, totally avoiding any eye contact with him.

"All the ambulances were full Rach, so we brought a few of the victims here in the fire trucks." Tyler replies who is still on a come-down from what happened.

"Oh ok, and you just happened to bring… Um … her?" Rachel questions him; this was one of those traps; women set them now and again to test men Tyler thinks to himself.

"Look Rachel, something happened back there, I don't know what exactly, but that girl was there too, I just have to ask her a few questions." A puzzled look falls over Rachel's face.

"Why Tyler, what happened to you tonight?"

"What did you see?" Rachel asks in a concerned manor. Tyler, not knowing how to answer mutters the words,

"I saw something, someone even, I swear to God Rachel, I know it sounds crazy but behind this guys eye's I could see my dad!"

Rachel falls silent for a moment before bowing her head.

"No Tyler, that isn't crazy. Sometimes we feel things, even see things that gives us a little hope. They're not always real, but they are real to us,"

Rachel sympathises before turning her head to the side.

"No Rachel, this was real, I swear to God,"

"It was him!" Tyler protests as he regains his confidence.

Rachel looks at Tyler whilst biting her lower lip.

"Are you alright Rach?" Tyler asks as he places his hands on her shoulders.

"Yeah, it's just…" Rachel pauses momentarily

"Well, my whole life I've always had this feeling…" Pausing again in embarrassment she turns her head before continuing.

Tyler listens on in silence, raising his hands to stroke her face when their eyes finally meet.

Giving Rachel the confidence to continue Tyler expresses a look of understanding.

"I've always had this overwhelming feeling that nothing could hurt me, a feeling of comfort."

"I've always believed that I had a guardian angel," Rachel opens up, slightly embarrassed. An uneasy silence falls between the two before another loud thud echoes through out the room.

From the streets a lot more victims start pouring in.

"Look Tyler, you really have to go,"

"I have patients that need me." Rachel tells him hurriedly as she begins to feel the pressure once more.

"Yeah, sure Rach, I understand," Tyler weakly replies whilst slowly dropping his hands down by his sides. As the young firefighter makes his way out of the ER, he remembers Rachel's words and how she spoke of a *guardian angel.*

Walking backwards Tyler's eyes can't leave Rachel's even as people rush between them blocking their view of each other, he feels a sparkle. Even if there eyes only met for a second he feels like the luckiest guy alive.

Leaving the hospital he can't help but feel fiery inside; as he hops in his car he sees an old lady walking her dog, he sits in the car for a few seconds relaying tonight's event over in his head before casting his mind back once more…

***

'What do I do, what do I do?' Tyler thinks to himself as he holds on to the branch for grim death.

"Don't worry boy, I'm coming, I'm coming." Tyler stresses towards the dog whilst analysing the tree working out what best to do. A few seconds later Rex begins to flap wildly as a slight breeze rustles the leaves around him causing them both to panic. Tyler decides to climb higher using the branches as his ladder as he does he also looses his balance and slips through two thick branches, thankfully managing to latch on to another branch as he falls.

Mr Peabody looks out his window at the commotion.

"Well would you look at that, they seem to be having fun." Mr Peabody mutters to himself whilst rushing back to the toilet.

Now extremely distressed Tyler manages to pull himself onto the branch he had grasped on the way down, resting momentarily before making one last attempt to save Rex.

"Go on Son, you can do it." Mason said into himself while watching on from his kitchen window. Unknown to Tyler Mason was there, just in case he needed him, but Mason had faith in his Son and let him continue on his own.

"Easy boy, don't move." Tyler whispered whilst inching his way ever closer to Rex. Another breeze made its way through the tree causing the branches to swing a little harder this time, causing Rex to flap once more, but this time he slipped out through two branches holding on with only his two front legs. Tyler knew that Rex couldn't hold on for ever and at that he closed his eyes and made a leap of faith. Time seemed to stand still as Tyler leapt through the air, at the same time Rex's front legs gave up and he to started falling. To Tyler's surprise, he felt the coarse hair of Rex through his fingers causing him to open his eyes.

"Now I've got you," Tyler thought to himself, but only then realised that he was now the victim, as he fell through the branches he clutched Rex tightly in his arms, again the moment appeared timeless until what felt like a warm giant cushioned his fall.

Opening his eyes Tyler couldn't see the man that had saved him due to the sunlight behind him, but he could feel who it was. Mason had let Tyler go so far on his own, far enough to see if his Son had what it took to follow his dreams.

21

In the warmth of the Dragons den, an angry Scapatechi listens as his dearest son explains the night's events and of the dark firefighter's intervention. Hearing the news, Scapatechi clenches his fists tightly, and then uncontrollably slams them into the desk in front of him.

"It was him again father, it's as if this guy is everywhere, every time we move he's on our back, I mean he's like a ghost or something."

As Flynt continues, one the mindless goons from the rear of the office pipes up,

"We're going to have to take care of this fire freak once and for all boss." The brainless goons comment was heard by Flynt and Scapatechi and at that moment the room fell silent. Scapatechi looks towards him with what appears to be devil eyes and the goon gets the message to keep his mouth shut. After a few dry seconds Scapatechi continues.

"This firefighter has been a thorn in my side for too many years."

"Tell me my son, if you can't hurt someone what do you do?" Scapatechi asks with a sinister smile.

Flynt still beaten and bruised from the alley fight with the firefighter looks at Scapatechi with a half smile.

"That's easy sir, you go after their nearest and dearest," he mumbles with a bloody lip. Scapatechi, now a little more relaxed walks towards the roaring open fire. Flynt looks on eagerly awaiting for his father's advice.

"My contacts in the force tell me that this freak firefighter has a soft spot for a young lady doctor,"

"Apparently he's been watching her back for some time now, so you can imagine, if we get her, we'll get him!" Scapatechi divulges. To Scapatechi's surprise the annoying goon pipes up once more,

"All we need is her details boss."

Without hesitation Scapatechi lifts his cold gun from his coat pocket, pointing it directly at the mouthy goon he opens fire; without even looking he shoots him twice in the stomach. With a surprisingly calm tone Scapatechi asks the now dead goon,

"Did I ask for you're opinion?"

Reaching down, Scapatechi pulls out some papers from his mahogany desk drawer and holds them for a while before handing the documents to Flynt. Flynt studies the documents under the glow of the roaring fire for a few seconds and as he does so his facial expression changes.

"Something wrong Son?" Scapatechi asks with a puzzled glare in his eye.

"No sir, everything is just fine," Flynt assures him.

"We won't have any problem with operation Midtown will we?" Scapatechi asks rhetorically.

"Of course not sir, everything is above board," echoes Flynt. Flynt recognizes the girl in the photo immediately.

'There you are,' he ponders to himself. For years Flynt had dreamt of this moment of finally tracking down his sister; well he didn't think for a second that it would be Scapatechi himself who would unknowingly be the one to reveal her identity.

For as long as Flynt can remember he has blamed his family so much for what happened, he hated Rachel for the mere fact that their parents loved her more than him. Through the years his jealousy turned to rage and his rage eventually turned to hate, creating a bitter and twisted dark mobster. Flynt leaves Scapatechi's office with his own agenda that evening. Two other high level mobsters automatically follow, but the dark loaner turns and with a look of insanity says,

"No, I'll get this bitch on my own!"

'Two birds with the one stone,' he thinks to himself.

The two mobsters stand at the door looking on in disbelief as they watch Flynt disappear into the shadows.

"That guy gives me the creeps," one of the mobsters whisper as he lights up a cigarette, the other agrees.

Making its way in from the shadows, a squad car carries Frank Lombardo towards the old fire station with speed. Swinging into the stations parking lot Lombardo abandons his car and then makes his way to the door.

"Open up guys, it's me, Lombardo," he whales.

"I'm coming, I'm coming!" Dale replies before unlatching the steel door. Once inside the station Lombardo lashes into an uncontrollable rage.

"What the hell happened in hell's kitchen?" Dale is now feeling the pressure as he is unable to answer, thankfully during the heightened questioning Dale notices Mason coming towards him.

"Jesus Christ Mason, what the hell happened to you?" Lombardo now directing his attention towards Mason's scorched appearance.

"Don't ask," laughs a busted up Mason, his humour calming the situation.

"I thought you said Midtown was the target?" Mason says accusingly as he walks past the men.

"Jesus Mason, I don't know, I just don't know!"

"They have killed Peratski, he was clubs owner; the one you were at tonight."

"They must have found out about him informing the department, damn it!" Lombardo sounds defeatist and extremely worried.

"Loose lips, sink ships," offers Dale as he lifts his coffee.

"Yeah, it seems so."

"Shit, he was our only lead," blasts Lombardo.

"I think I saw him Lombardo!" Mason exclaims.

"Saw who..." Lombardo enquires.

There is a brief pause,

"His son, that's who," Dale adds breaking the silence.

Lombardo knows that the city needs Hope right now and the introduction of Mason's lost son could jeopardise everything.

"Look Mason, let's keep our minds on the job right now, Scapatechi and his crew are up to something, something big! By the way just before Peratski was hit he dropped a line to the chief, telling him that something crazy was happening very soon. After it's all over, there will be plenty of time to play happy families."

Leaping from the stairs, Mason squares right up to Lombardo, face to face.

"Look Lombardo, you might know a lot of things in this city, but the one thing you don't know is me! What I've lost!" Mason shouts forcefully. Lombardo knows he may have over stepped the mark when addressing his family, so he took a step back for a few minutes to let the dust settle.

"Look guys there's no sense us fighting amongst ourselves, especially when Scapatechi is out there! Its time for a little unity, don't you think?" Dale reminds the two men with an honourable tone.

"Ok Mason put it there my friend," Lombardo says while extending his hand in search for Mason's. The two men look at each other for a few seconds before Mason clutches Lombardo's hand hard and firm causing a thud which echoes through out the station.

"Now that's the spirit guys," an enthusiastic Dale shouts.

A well-disguised Flynt sits on a hospital bed keeping his partly opened eye on the look out for his lost but not forgotten sister.

"There you are," he mutters to himself as he catches a glimpse of Rachel beyond the water dispenser.

Biding his time before she makes her way down the isle towards him,

"Aw, doctor, please, I'm in real pain over here." He moans cunningly.

"I'm so sorry sir, I'll be with you as soon as I can," Rachel responds as she signs off another patient.

She is still rushed off her feet with the very heavy work load from the nightclub fire, however Rachel senses something strangely familiar about this guy, and something draws her to him. Before she knows it she finds herself tending his wounds before finally plucking up the courage to ask.

"Do I know you from somewhere, you're strangely familiar?" Rachel asks, feeling a little embarrassed she waits until the stranger replies,

"Funny I was going to ask you the same question!"

Unaware of the situation Rachel continues to make friendly small talk with the bruised stranger completely unaware of his true identity. The more she looks at him the more she recognises him, and in disbelief she drops her stethoscope and takes a step back,

"Michael, it can't be."

"I thought you were dead!"

She could barely speak the words; her heart misses a beat before she suddenly feels a rush of blood streaming towards her face.

"Well as you can see I'm not dead, no thanks to you,"

"Oh, The name is Flynt, Michael died along time ago sister," he says in a menacing tone.

As Rachel heard him say the name Flynt, she immediately recognises it from newspaper and news bulletins.

"You Monster, you're with the Scapatechi crew!" She rants. She had aided many of Scapatechi's victims through the years and it made her sick to think that her own brother was part of it.

"Well after all, he is my father," he whispers, his words send shivers down her spin.

Rachel is speechless and can't believe that her brother is still alive after all these years, and more so what he has become; she feels physically sick.

Without warning, another patient barges through the doors grabbing the attention of the other doctors; it's at this moment Flynt takes advantage of the distraction and nudges Rachel with his concealed gun.

"You know the drill sister, the easy way, or the hard way, it's your call!"

Flynt continues to push the gun deep into Rachel's side causing her to grind her teeth with pain. Just when Flynt orders Rachel to stand up Dr Whiley barges over to quiz her about some mixed up files.

"This isn't a good time Whiley!" Rachel pleads.

"Oh yeah Rachel, when is a good time for you?" Whiley whines.

"Or maybe it's just because it's me, I thought we were…" Before Whiley can even finish his sentence Flynt raises his gun and smashes it into Whiley's face sending the cocky doctor to the ground with a thud.

"You broke my nose you asshole!" Whiley screams in agony.

"As the girl said Doc, maybe another time…"

Flynt smiles as he forces Rachel out of the hospital at gun point leaving Dr Whiley on his knees covered in blood.

22

Tyler now speeding down the winding back streets of New York on his motorcycle tries to clear his head. He is looking for answers, looking for reason. As he replays the vision of the mysterious firefighter over and over in his mind he rides on finding himself on some familiar ground,

'Jesus, it's Franklin Street,' he thinks to himself. As he becomes aware of his surroundings, child hood memories come flooding back.

"It can't be," Tyler whispers while looking on with amazement.

"It's got to be around here somewhere!" He reminds himself. A few turns later Tyler is met with a hidden piece of history; there it was, just off Franklin Street, the old station. Although it was a little darker with less life it was exactly how he remembered it,

'Could it be coincidence, tonight's events and now this?' Tyler circles it over in his mind before making a decision to enter the stations parking lot.

"Nothing ventured, nothing gained right." Tyler whispers to himself.

He wheels his motorcycle into the lot placing his helmet on the seat. While doing so he notices a beat out squad car partly in the shadows, thinking nothing much of it he stands back and gasps with excitement, mixed a little fear as he gazes at this forgotten building.

Tyler touches the red bricked wall with his hand then sliding it across towards the door he grasps for the door handle, taking a deep breath he can't help but embrace the nostalgia.

***

His tiny hand in his fathers big hand, made Tyler feel secure and safe. As they entered the station Tyler couldn't wait to tell Dale of his heroic story, saving Mr Peabody's dog then falling from the tree with it clutched tightly in his arms, the feeling was truly overwhelming for the young hero. Now he could be just like his Dad, the feeling of being respected and listened to was as a good feeling as making a home-run in front of his school pals in a high profile baseball game. Dale was like an uncle to Tyler; he always enjoyed it when his parents would have Dale around for Thanksgiving lunch and Christmas dinner, the good old days Tyler recalled. Letting go of his father's hand Tyler raced towards Dale's workshop passing the other guys on his way ensuring to say hi as he passed them. Nearing the workshop Tyler came to a sudden halt, noticing that the workshop door was shut tight, he hesitated in entering; he didn't exactly know why but he sensed something uneasy from the work shop, something strange. He crept closer to the door where he found a crack in the wooden surround, he knew it was wrong to pry on people but something deep down pulled him into towards it. He peered through the crack in the workshop door for a few second before noticing a strange figure through what appeared to be a cindering smoke. Tyler couldn't understand what he was seeing; as the smoke cleared a monstrous form emerged, though it seemed lifeless, as if just hanging and not yet awake. Tyler's heart seems to fill his throat then to his amazement he noticed Dale walk out from behind the giant figure with a blow torch which now held a low blue light. Turning in his heels Tyler made a dash for it though he doesn't get far as he ran straight into his fathers leg, his heart was pounding and his lip was shaking with fear. Suddenly the door opened and Dale slowly emerged from the darkness.

✳✳✳

Inside the old station Mason, Dale and Lombardo hears the door handle turn.

"Out of sight everyone!" Mason whispers. As the door opens, the adventurous young firefighter enters and can't help but feel at home here. This place brought back some amazing memories, although the more Tyler looked around the more he sensed something was up, he couldn't help but continue to investigate this familiar place and from what he could see it was as if the place had been lived in or something.

"Hello, Is there anyone here?" His voice echoes before falling silent.

Before Tyler can ask again, a voice from the shadows echoes back across the room,

"That kind of depends on who's asking kid?"

Looking in the direction of the voice, Tyler steps back in shock.

"Who's there?" He shouts bravely.

"I'll say it again kid, that depends on who's asking!" The voice from the shadows was deep, gruff, though Tyler found it strangely peaceful.

"My name is Tyler Hope!" He calls now feeling uneasy. The Station fills with an atmospheric silence, seconds later the shadowy figure who was answering Tyler's call steps half into the light.

"My Son, Is that you?" The dark figure asks.

Tyler's entire body shakes as his father's voice runs through him. He is now more confused than ever. Eventually plucking up the courage to respond,

"D-Dad, is that you?"

"Wait a minute what the hell?"

"My dad is dead!" Tyler shouts his voice laced with emotion.

Turning on his heels, Tyler decides to run from the station, however he doesn't get very far as he runs straight into Lombardo's chest.

"Easy boy," requests Lombardo who tries to put Tyler at ease.

"Let me go man, let me go." Tyler demands.

A third voice spoke grasping Tyler's attention, Tyler's mind runs in a thousand directions, fearing the worst he begins to struggle more and more. Not trusting the situation or these strange men he looks towards the door were the third man stood. With his eyes latched onto the man he suddenly remembers, and then slowly, Tyler starts to calm down.

"Dale, is that you?" Tyler gasps whilst shrugging from Lombardo's firm grip.

"How are you little Tyler?"

"Though you're not so little anymore are you?" Dale chuckles; trying to break the ice.

"Release him Lombardo; I think he's calm now!" Mason orders.

At Mason's request Lombardo releases Tyler who is still trying to keep his distance from them all. Shacking with adrenaline he makes his way to the back wall,

"Jesus Dale, what are you doing here, what is this shit man?" Tyler nervously asks.

Dale didn't quite know what to say, the only words he can think have were,

"Maybe your dad should be the one to answer that kid."

Tyler turns to the man who's is still partly hidden by shadows. The man steps out into the light revealing him-self. Both of them are equally as awe struck, speechless, and for a while the two just stare at each other. Tyler looks deep into this enormous roughed up firefighter's eyes, and then it hits him hard, he finally finds his dad beneath the harsh exterior of his super human body; the eyes never lie!

"D-D-Dad… Is it really you?" Tyler stutters, his eyes now wide with disbelief and his mind staggers with countless thoughts of reason.

Tears for a Son

Mason's eyes fill up with a tear as the sheer sight of his only son numbs his warm heart; it was truly overwhelming for both of them.

"Jesus Son, come here!" Mason steps forward reaching out for his Son.

"I missed you Dad,"Tyler gasps as they embrace each other. A few seconds later Tyler's emotions change.

"You left us."

"How do you think me and mom felt?" Tyler shouts before he starts punching his Dad's chest repeatedly.

Although the blows had really no effect on Mason he could feel the pain on the inside, and at that Tyler broke down like a boy as his Dad held him tightly.

"I'm truly sorry my son, forgive me…" Mason whispers.

Tyler looks up into his Dad's eyes and mutters, "I'm just glad you're still alive Dad."

"I hate to break up the party guys but there's a god damn maniac out there who's going to mess this city up real bad!" Blasts Lombardo; He is pretty cold about the whole family thing as he is only interested in good old school police work. Everyone knew this, deep down Lombardo knew it too, this is why he never married, but he always blamed the lack of good women in New York.

"I'm going to head back to the precinct to see if there are any more leads. After you guy's get acquainted just sit tight and wait for my call." Lombardo orders as he walks down towards his squad car. Coincidentally, just as he opens his car door the C.B. starts to crackle.

"All units… I repeat… all units." Rushing to screw up the volume, Lombardo lifts the C.B. and patiently waits for the message.

"There's been a possible kidnapping at Liberty City's Hospital. The victim is a Caucasian female, blonde hair by the name of Dr. Rachel Wood's… We've got two units chasing a suspect black car to the Midtown area".

At that, Lombardo pulls the car nearer the station. The room stands silent for a moment and before they can muster a reaction more crackles come from the C.B. It starts buzzing, though the voice isn't clear, Lombardo knows who it is. He turns the tuning knob to find a lower frequency so they can make out the message.

"Lombardo, if you're out there… know this! Before dawn your good city will be no more than a memory. It will be a hot night in Manhattan! Oh one other thing, tell your friend the freak firefighter that we've got his little angel, and if that he even thinks of intervening, well, you're going to just have to use your imagination." With that the C.B. falls silent.

The voice of Scapatechi leaves a chilling echo through out the old station.

"That Bastard!" Mason roars.

His words are closely followed with a ferocious punch to a wall causing pieces of brick and dust to fly.

"OK who the hell was that on the C.B, what's going on here?" Tyler yells his voice agitated.

Mason did not respond, however Lombardo did answer Tyler's call.

"That was the voice of Scapatechi, a twisted maniac who's going to kill a lot of people, oh and he's got his grubby hands on Rachel," Lombardo continues.

"Wait a minute, Rachel, the doctor Rachel? What the hell does she have to do with all this?" Tyler yells who by now is in a state of panic.

"She has a lot to do with this, that sick animal is using her to get to me," Mason adds.

"Why the hell would he do that?"

"Dad?" Tyler asks, now in frenzy. He can't understand what Rachel had got to do with all this. Mason walks back over towards his son. Not knowing what his father was about to say Tyler can do nothing but stand and listen.

"I saved her along time ago Son, it was the night the 'Blue Angels' fell, down in dockland," Tyler listens on with eager ears.

"There was just something about her that night, I found your sisters spirit in her and it was that spirit that gave me the strength to keep going through the dark years." The emotional moment is interrupted by Dale,

"That's right Tyler, and he's been watching her back ever since," he adds. Lombardo knows of the growing romance between Rachel and Tyler, though decides to keep the information to himself for now at least, and as he knew time was against them and didn't want to waste anymore on senseless emotional small talk.

"Time to ride boys," orders a now anxious Detective.

Tyler still vexed at tonight's events takes a few moments to pull him-self together,

'Jesus Rachel,' Tyler thinks to him self. It finally hits him, his girl is in trouble, and it's time to move.

"If that maniac succeeds, this city is doomed guys." Dale expresses.

"I wouldn't worry about him succeeding Dale!" Mason replies as he reaches for his razor sharp axe.

"I am sure this city has enough good men left, wouldn't you agree fellows?" Mason asks both Lombardo and Tyler with a half smile. Understanding his dad's thinking, Tyler returns a half smile and throw's him the keys.

"What the hell is this Son?" Mason asks surprisingly.

"You'll see Dad." Tyler confidently responds before heading out the back door with Lombardo.

Tyler and Lombardo jump into the beat up squad car. Before they speed off into the dark streets Lombardo suggests that they meet in midtown just after they make a few stops along the way, leaving Mason standing in the yard in full view of a huge kick ass motorcycle which is parked in front of him.

"Yeah, you got my taste kid, not bad, not bad at all," Mason laughs to him self before heading back into the station.

23

Squads of Scapatechi's goons make their way through the Midtown streets terrorising everyone in their path.

"Leave Midtown tonight..." Yell the grimy goons.

Scores of people hit the road, trying their hardest to get out of harms way.

"Help us, help us!" Plead the women and children to the patrolling Police units; however when the police cars roll up they are met with merciless gang members who automatically open fire with their Tommy guns. Before long there are major shootouts on most street corners, Midtown is in pandemonium...

Thirty floors up, in an empty office with only a few chairs around Rachel helplessly looks on as the pure streets of Midtown turn to a war zone.

"My God, what's happening?" She gasps in disbelief.

She can't believe her eyes at the sheer heartless actions of the goons, when suddenly her attention is diverted from the streets below as she hears the door being unlocked. Waiting for it to open, Rachel now terrified for her life looks on, then to her surprise the notorious mobster Scapatechi enters. Rachel looks right at him for a few seconds before turning her back on him.

"I should have known that this is your handy work!" Rachel yells at him in a sarcastic tone.

Unresponsive to Rachel's words Scapatechi continues,

"Glad you could join us Rachel; however I won't be around to watch the fireworks!"

Scapatechi has a smug look on his face, quite harrowing.

"Oh and we're going to take care of that firefighter for once and for all, who is going to save you now precious Rachel?" Scapatechi laughs before reaching for his victory cigar.

"What the hell are you talking about?"

"You mean Tyler Hope, what the hell he has got to do with all this?" Rachel questions.

Scapatechi observes her with an obviously puzzled look,

"No not Tyler, Mason!" He yells.

As these words pass his lips, the pieces started to fit together causing Rachel to fall silent for a few seconds; Rachel's mom always told her of the man that saved her, the fallen angel...

'Wait a minute he died that night.' Rachel recalls, though she couldn't ever explain that feeling of warmth that she always carried.

"Could it be true?" She ponders for a moment before her emotions take over.

"You Monster," she screams whilst making a dash for the insane mobster, her heart fills with rage. But before she could even get a swing at him, Scapatechi hits her across the mouth with the back of his hand sending the helpless damsel to the ground with a thump. Just before she passes out she can see the hazy figure of another man enter the room,

"M-M-Michael?" She stutters before her eyes close; she was out cold.

The precinct is now buzzing with calls with many police officers hustling around questioning prostitutes and interrogating bad guys.

"Where the hell are you Lombardo? Midtown's been overrun and we haven't got the manpower to deal with this shit," shouts an extremely frustrated commissioner down the phone. Just as he finishes what he is saying a light vibration shakes the precinct.

"What the hell is that?" The commissioner asks as he stares at his shaking coffee mug. The buzzing precinct soon grows silent as the vibrations grow.

"It's an earthquake," shouts a saucy handcuffed prostitute.

"No it couldn't be," replies the arresting officer as he takes a drag of his cigarette. The officer is right, the vibration was no earthquake; however to his surprise it is squads of Fire engines alongside countless police cars and ambulances moving towards midtown in a huge convoy, they move together as one causing the city streets to shake.

"Well would you look at that!" The commissioner gasps in astonishment before gulping down the rest of his black coffee.

"Now there's something you don't see everyday," another cop expresses.

The solidarity of the 911 services of the New York, working together to fight terror was in the hearts of everyone. The unstoppable heroes make their way up towards Midtown stopping at every fire house and precinct on their way. At the front of the convoy was Tyler and Lombardo, both wearing stereotype clothing to suit their rolls; Tyler with boots fire trousers, white vest, red braces with his helmet under his arm and Lombardo with his long beige trench coat, white shirt, suit trousers along with his badge and gun shown on his belt line. It truly is an amazing site. As the strong convoy approaches Lombardo's precinct he pulls up to the steps and gets out; his aim is to gather up and organise any free men he can find.

"What were you saying about man power commissioner?" Lombardo asks before pulling a huge grin.

The commissioner, still not showing any gratitude, roars,

"It's about time Lombardo, no time for coffee breaks around here," He blasts just before he snatches a large mug of coffee out of a near by officers hand. Staggering to his feet as if he was on a caffeine rush, he lets out another loud yell.

"Ok men, you heard Lombardo, let's get moving," he eventually gets the attention of everyone in the precinct. Lombardo and the commissioner look at each other for a second and with a half smile the commissioner nods to Lombardo and says,

"Thanks Frank I knew you would be the one."

Out front Tyler notices a familiar engine to his left.

"Well I'll be…" He says to himself.

"Lombardo, I'll meet you in Midtown," he shouts before making his way across to the engine.

"Yeah sure kid, just don't be late!" Lombardo replies.

"Short notice Tyler, but we made it amigo!" JJ says as he holds out his hand for Tyler to grasp before climbing aboard.

"Thought you guys would never get here!" Tyler jokes as he jumps into the front seat.

"What the hell is going on Tyler?" Sandy demands.

"Not sure Sandy, all I know is that maniac Scapatechi is planning to destroy Midtown, we don't know how yet but we're going to stop him!" Tyler bravely responds.

"Oh yeah new guy, and how would you know that?" One of the Torelli brothers asks.

"Let's just say an Angel told me!" Tyler replies with a look of sincerity.

24

The tail of his fire jacket blows in the wind as a motorcycle carries the lone firefighter towards Midtown. Mason roars through the now empty streets with his mind running in all directions, but has only one definite purpose; Rachel…

Deep underground a team of Scapatechi's goons set the timers on countless detonators for three minutes before scrambling to the surface. With the purpose being to ignite the rivers of oil beneath Midtown causing it to burn from beneath, allowing the insane Scapatechi to rebuild it as his own. As the villains emerge from the open manhole to join the others, they notice faint blue lights from the distance.

"What the hell is that?" One of the goons shrieks.

They are stunned to see the lights as they assumed all police resources would be stretched across Midtown due to their sporadic violence. Regrouping, they continue to engage in shootouts with the existing police forces bringing absolute terror to the city.

Meanwhile on the thirtieth floor Rachel comes to, finding herself tied to a chair facing Flynt, her head still aches and her vision is still a little blurred; however she can make out the man in front of her.

"Michael, what is this?"

"What are you doing?" Rachel asks, now very frightened and frantically trying to free her arms from the ropes.

"Sister Rachel, Oh how I have waited for this moment with you." Flynt replies in a tone which is certainly sadistic.

"Are you crazy Michael?"

"Let me go, you're sick, I can help you!" Rachel screams at her deranged brother. Michael strikes Rachel across the face causing her head to turn; he then grasps her throat and growls,

"Your fault; it's all your fault!" Rachel, now turning red, coughs…

"You're hurting me!"

Taking a step back Flynt looks at Rachel were he notices her gasping for air.

"Can you imagine what it was like?"

"Getting beaten every night by that drunken animal… Can you!" Flynt now shouts in an aggressive tone.

"It's ok, I understand Michael you're safe now." Rachel reassures him in sympathetic tones, thinking she is finally getting through to him she tilts her head in empathy when suddenly he raises one of his hands and says…

"Michael is gone, though Flynt has been born!"

No sooner than these words pass his lips, as if from nowhere his raised hand holds a warm flame.

"Oh my god, what are you?" Rachel gasps in disbelief.

As the convoy approaches they are met with chaos.

"Holy shit… Would you look at that?" JJ gasps in astonishment as he notices countless thugs running wild with Tommy guns.

"If I get my hands on that creep Scapatechi I am going to kill him!" Sandy shouts, her voice laced with hatred.

"Not before me, he's got his hands on Rachel!" Tyler bravely adds.

"Wait a minute, Rachel from the Tavern Rachel?" Kastle shouts in a confused voice.

"Yes my Rachel." Tyler replies. Sandy does not respond.

On the streets more violence erupts, the fire fights breaking out between police officers and Scapatechi's men get fierce causing the cops to take cover behind some of the fire engines.

"Ok, move in," orders Lombardo as he walks up front. Undeterred by the flying bullets the Detective calmly lights up a cigar sending a no fear signal to the bad guys. Slowly but surely the cops move in, pushing the trigger happy goons back inch by inch.

"That's it men, no fear," growls Lombardo. A few rookie cops look at each other in disbelief,

"That Lombardo is nuttier than squirrel shit," they say to each other before reloading their weapons.

"Yeah I've noticed, or maybe it's just that he really is crazy," the other rookie responds. At that moment the detonators ignite the rivers of oil beneath the streets, turning it rapidly into a river of uncontrollable, belching dragon's breath. Thundering vibrations echo from below, causing the shootouts between the good guys and bad guys to stop.

"What is this shit?" A rookie cop gasps in horror.

Within seconds bursts of wild fire shoot up from below, every manhole cover and grate in Midtown flips up about eighty feet into the air followed by columns of wild fire.

"Take cover!" Lombardo yells from the top of his voice.

At Lombardo's warning every one ducks down for cover; even the goons scamper as the heavy round slabs of iron fall from the sky, pulverising everything they land on.

"Well I'll be damned!" Lombard mutters as one of the iron grates smashes right through his already beat out squad car.

"I loved that car..." He moans, paying no attention to the uncontrollable bursts of fire; a situation which you could easily imagine the end of the world to be like.

"Ok men lets regroup," commands Lombardo who is by now totally pissed off.

The firefighters quickly assemble; dodging their way through flames and bullets under the protection of armed cops they start the preparations for one hell of a fire fight.

"That crazy bastard was right!" Lombardo shouts over the roaring sound of gun fire.

"Oh yeah and what was that?" The commissioner asks in an agitated tone.

"It's going to be a hot night in Midtown Manhattan!" Lombardo replies whilst shooting off his gun.

Through the smoke, Mason emerges like a true hero, steering his motor cycle around burning cars and uncontrollable flame pockets bursting from the underground, finally reaching the front line where he catches sight of the unimaginable carnage that's taking place.

'You took your time Mason,' Lombardo thinks to himself.

As Mason passes the squads of cops and firefighters he remains silent and consistent, catching the attention of most guys on the ground, he continues.

"What the hell was that?" The baffled commissioner yells.

"You got me!" Lombardo replies, trying to look surprised.

"Get him," roars one of the goons.

At that command the goons turn in the direction of Mason opening fire on him, however undeterred by the bullets Mason keeps his aim on the gang, and now at great speed he accelerates to a greater speed towards them before jumping from the motorcycle with grace sending it straight into the gang crushing them against a red brick wall like bowling pins.

"STRIKE!" Mason shouts sarcastically, as he watches the last one fall he latches onto an above fire escape before climbing upwards to the buildings rooftop, looking down on the once pure streets of Midtown he can't believe his eyes.

'My God, what has that maniac done?' He ponders in disbelief.

'Revelations,' he whispers harrowingly as he notices the streets of fire blaze uncontrollably below him.

On the ground the squads of firefighters and police units gasp with astonishment, wondering who the phantom figure was. It isn't long before one of them works it out.

"It's him!"

"It's the fallen angel," one of the proby firefighters shouts out with excitement.

"Bullshit kid, everyone knows he's only a myth!" Lombardo snaps with his fingers crossed behind his back.

"That was probably one of those low flying buzzard hawks or something," he adds whist delving into the pocket of his trench coat feeling for more bullets.

Standing tall on the buildings rooftop, the warm wind blows his long fire jacket back revealing his true form.

"Jesus Mason, why can't you stay out of sight?" Lombardo mutters to himself shaking his head as he notices all of the young firefighters looking towards the sky at the mysterious silhouette.

Across the way Tyler's fire crew are battling three flaming cars when someone shouts aloud,

"Look, up there, it's him!"

Caught by the mans words Tyler and his crew cast their eyes towards the roof top and look on in wonderment when they catch sight of the towering silhouette of a firefighter who stands tall; watching over them like a dark angel.

From the rooftop Mason looks upon them like a Sheppard to his sheep, his blood boils as he watches on when they become surrounded by the fires of hell.

"My God, what has that maniac done?" He asks himself in disbelief.

Now frantically trying to work out a plan of action he notices the city's water treatment plant to the west,

'I've got to get a closer look!' he thinks to himself before making direction towards it. Leaping from roof top to roof top Mason makes his way towards the water plant narrowly missing towering flames that seem to shoot up from below like in Middle East oil fields, he continues onward into the night like a silent panther in a concrete jungle. Although closer inspection tells him that the plant is now under heavy guard by Scapatechi's henchmen.

"Damn it, I'm going to need a little help on this one!" Mason considers though he knows time is against him.

Back on the ground the brave police officers continue to exchange bullets with the mob, pushing them back down the Avenue, allowing the firefighters to steadily battle the uncontrollable flames that continue to reach out for them.

Meanwhile back on the thirtieth floor, Rachel is still trying relentlessly to talk sense to her estranged brother. Now terrified by the freakish power that he possesses she pleads with him to untie her.

"Michael, please, it doesn't have to be this way!" Rachel pleads, her voice quivering.

However, her psychotic brother has other plans for the evening, involving some pyrokenetic action. Moving towards Rachel, Flynt raises his two hands creating a flame in each of them causing Rachel to scream uncontrollably.

"Please help me, anybody!" Undeterred by Rachel's pleas, Flynt continues taunting her with the fire; the sick animal seems to be enjoying himself when suddenly he is interrupted by a voice over the C.B.

"You better get down here Flynt, it's getting hot," sneers the goon on the other end of the crackling C.B.

Rachel looks on with a slight feeling of relief as Flynt extinguishes his flames and gets ready to leave the room.

"Don't go away now Rachel, you wouldn't want to miss the fireworks, oh and if the fire from below doesn't get you don't worry, I will return!" Flynt expresses with a cruel tone before kicking the C.B. off table sending it crashing to the floor.

Rachel looks down at the blazing streets of Midtown; she can't believe her eyes, she knows that her only chance of contact is the beaten C.B. She tries relentlessly to free herself from the ropes and reach out for help, but the ropes are too tight leaving her helpless and alone were she kicks and screams uncontrollably praying for a miracle. Just as Flynt makes his way down through the building, it catches fire causing a small explosion in the lobby.

"It looks like the end of the line for you sister!" Flynt echoes as he makes his way into the flaming streets of Midtown.

Mason, now back on the violent smouldering streets approaches the squad of 911 service men. Undeterred by the fire and bullets around him he keeps his vision steady and walks straight up to the front line.

"Lombardo, were the hell are you?" Mason demands, his eyes scanning everywhere. The faces of the shocked police and firefighters alike reflect their disbelief as the watch this huge entity roar towards them.

"Over here Mason!" Lombardo shouts from behind his now busted up squad car whilst blasting off the last few rounds from his gun.

"Where is my son?" Mason roars with a gallant look on his face. Before he could get out another word scores of bullets whiz by over head causing everyone to duck, however Mason and Lombardo stands tall ignoring the goon's taunts.

"He's over there, dealing with those burning cars!" Lombardo answers as he reloads his gun.

"Grab him when you're finished with taking out the trash and meet me over there!"

Across the way in a derelict hardware store Mason, Lombardo and Tyler now stand together.

"Jesus Dad, we're fighting an un winnable battle,"

"We have no chance!" Tyler thunders in a very frustrated tone as he throws his fire jacket to the ground.

"He's right Mason, it's looking bleak out there!" Lombardo agrees, then as if from nowhere he aims his gun out the window towards a group of goons blasting off another six shots.

"We've got every chance!" Mason disputes whilst looking at Lombardo as if he were insane. Lifting his jacket from the ground Tyler opens up with emotion.

"Look around you guys, the city is falling in around us and yet these men out here still fight,"

"With courage and honour they fight!"

"Doesn't that tell you something?"

Lombardo's courage was renewed when he saw what Tyler meant, and deep down he knew that there was a lot of honour on the streets tonight.

"So what's your plan Dad?" Tyler asks with a glimmer of hope in his eye.

Lombardo and Tyler listen intently as Mason explains the plan of action.

"What we need is an opening, a safe route to the city's water treatment plant, although there's only one problem."

"What's that?" Lombardo asks.

"There is a heavy guard presence there, can you do it Lombardo?" Mason presses him for a positive response.

"Of course I can Mason, I just need a little time!" Lombardo responds even though he knows that time was one thing they had very little of.

"What about Rachel?" Tyler asks his voice noticeably agitated. Father and son look at each other with a knowing look for a few seconds before the commissioner busts through the door of the hardware store.

"All right which one of you all is Tyler?" Yells the commissioner in an aggressive tone causing the veins in his neck and head to appear like hot pumping tubes of fire. Tyler's heart skips a beat when he hears his name being called in this manor.

"That would be me!" Tyler replies with a curious tone.

"Then get your ass out to what's left of Lombardo's piece of shit car, there is some broad on the C.B. calling your name!" Scanning the room the commissioner notices Mason who is again hidden in the shadows, his face only partly showing by the fierce red glow of the smouldering streets outside.

"Who the hell is this guy Lombardo?"

"Bigfoot with an axe,"

"Get your asses out here!" The commissioner bellows before kicking the door open and pulling his gun from his holster.

"Seems like a nice guy," Mason grunts before making his way towards Lombardo's car.

The sound of static comes through the C.B. in Lombardo's car. The streets are still in pandemonium but Tyler makes a dash for the car dodging threat of fire and bullets.

"Hello, can anyone hear me?" He shouts erratically before squeezing the switch repeatedly on the handset. A faint voice echoes from the static filled line causing Tyler to turn the knobs in despair.

"Hello, who the hell is this,"

"Is that you Rach?"

"Are you out there?" Tyler now becomes impatient he starts to roar into the speaker; Mason listens on from the shadowy doorway when suddenly the voice becomes a little clearer.

"Please, can any one hear me?"

"Rachel, are you all right?"

"Where the hell are you?" He asks, his voice now calming some more.

"Tyler, Thank God…"

"I'm trapped in the old Shymna building, I'm unsure of the floor; it's pretty far maybe the thirtieth." Rachel tells him, finding some composure and just relieved that she got to the C.B. in time.

"Just hold on Rachel, I'll be there as soon as I can!" Tyler promises before making a dash back towards the hardware store were he shouts to Mason and Lombardo,

"I know where she is!"

But to his surprise his father was already gone leaving him alone with Lombardo,

"That son of a bitch…" Tyler shouts, his voice laced with anger as he needs his father now more than ever. Lombardo looks on as Tyler kicks and punches the door of his car,

"Easy kid, that's my pride and joy you're busting up there." Lombardo yells as he pulls Tyler away from his car. Calming down he looks at Lombardo before a shadow from the fire catches his eye. The two men look at each other for a few seconds before Lombardo gives a nod,

"It's him…" Tyler whispers, his heart warms again when Mason arrives back with a bullet proof vest, handing it to Tyler before shielding Lombardo from a sudden burst of fire

"Damn that was close," Lombardo gasps, kneeling down to avoid anymore bullets or fire the three guys start putting their plan in motion.

25

Back on the wild smouldering streets, Lombardo hand picks a few good men from the various precincts to spearhead their way through Scapatechi's strong resistance.

"Listen up guys, our objective is to clear a path to the water treatment plant; just keep your heads down and your eyes open." Lombardo roars with a firm voice of leadership. At Lombardo's command the team of sharp shooters start moving towards the plant enabling the firefighters to follow close behind using their powers more efficiently to control the blazing streets. On the other side of the street, Father and Son stand before the fire crew exchanging a few words before parting paths.

"You find her Tyler and keep her safe I can see it in your eyes, you can do this!"

"Remember when you were a little boy and you asked me when you could go to work with me, well now is that time boy." Mason's encouraging words give his son the will and determination to save the woman he now realises he loves.

"What about you Dad?" Tyler asks whist strapping on the bullet proof vest.

"I'm going after Scapatechi, something I should have done a long time ago." At that Mason disappears into the flames.

Making his way towards his team Tyler dashes through the flames before he finds cover behind a beat out truck.

"Over here!" He shouts to the guys from behind an over turned ice truck, catching their attention he signals them over.

"What is it Tyler?" Sandy asks after she slides in under the truck, Tyler remains silent until the rest of the team make their way to the truck.

"Ok listen up guys, I know were she is,"

"But I need your help." A silence follows his words then they all gave Tyler a look of solidarity and honour.

"Let's do it!" Tyler adds with a half smile.

Inside the building the smoke is thick and heavy, every so often rogue flames shoot up from beneath. The Torelli brothers roll out the hoses and swiftly connect it up trying relentlessly to battle the flames at the foot of the staircase enabling Tyler to begin his assent to the thirtieth floor.

"Jesus Tyler this is suicide!" Screams JJ as he looks into the fiery abyss.

"Look JJ, I've got to do this,"

"I've got to save her!" Tyler replies with determination as he knows he has to save Rachel. JJ contemplates for a few seconds before Tyler holds out his hand, still unsure JJ hesitates for a moment before Tyler says,

"No hope, no glory man!" JJ raises his eyes locking them onto Tyler's.

"Ok brother I am with you all the way." JJ replies with a hint of honour in his eyes.

As they climb upwards a thundering sound bellows from above, Tyler looks at JJ with an unsettling look. Kastle and Sandy hold tight as the thundering heightens.

"It's probably nothing," JJ says convincingly, moving onwards he notices that the thunderous vibrations grow stronger this time accompanied by heavy thuds; the thuds continue consistently like a giants heart beat until a large section of staircase comes crashing down smashing everything in its path.

"Holy shit, everybody hold tight!" Tyler roars whilst diving from the falling ball of flaming concrete.

When the dust settles, Tyler notices huge voids behind him where JJ and the crew had been standing, causing Tyler to think the worst.

He starts yelling uncontrollably for his fallen comrades as he can't help but feel responsible. Falling to his knees Tyler starts to loose all hope when suddenly his radio starts to crackle.

"Tyler… It's JJ,"

"Come in!" JJ whispers in a beaten down faint voice.

Tyler can't believe his ears,

"What's going on down there, is everyone alright?" Tyler speedily responds.

"T…T…Tyler, We're trapped!"

"Is everyone alright?" Tyler persists.

"Everyone's here and yes still moving but not for long, the blaze is getting to strong, hurry!" JJ yells.

Bout thirty floors above Tyler's dilemma, Rachel is still eagerly trying to free her other arm from the ropes, but panics as she feels the effects of the nearing fire.

"Help me, please!" Rachel pleads. Right now a despondent look comes over Tyler's face. He knows JJ and the guys are in trouble, and he can just make out that the Torelli Brothers were also trapped. Tyler is faced with a terrible decision. Standing mid-way on the burning staircase, he looks down and then up?

'Jesus, what the hell do I do?' He thinks in despair.

Mason soon caught up with Lombardo's team who were in the midst of battling the trigger happy goons; trying their up most to ensure a safe passage for the fire department they continue the fire fight courageously.

"Lombardo, any sign of Scapatechi?" Mason queries.

"No not at all, though a few of our guys have spotted that crazy son of his about four blocks up ahead!" Lombardo replies after shielding his face from another burst of wild fire.

"Damn it, where the *Hell* is he!" Mason grunts whilst punching into his palm.

"One of Scapatechi's choppers has just landed on the Shymna building," the commissioner yells, who had just received word over his radio.

"That coward has been there all along!" Mason howls before turning his head back towards the Shymna building were notices the chopper lights circling its roof.

"There you are!" Mason divulges as he peers towards the red skies. After blasting off another few rounds Lombardo turns to Mason.

"Go on Mason you do what you've got to do, we can take it from hear." Lombardo affirms as he raises his heavy axe from his side.

"Are you sure you can handle it alone?" Mason asks as he looks across the fiery battlefields.

"What... kill all the bad guys take over the water plant and flush out the underground?"

"Piece of cake big guy," Lombardo yells sarcastically as he watches Mason disappear into the fiery streets of hell.

Back in the Shymna building Tyler is still contemplating his next move; however before he can make a decision, another thundering vibration begins to materialize close to where he stands. A crash from a nearby window sounds, and as if from nowhere a heavy shadow darts towards him. The shadow now grows larger until Tyler's heart fills with hope as the image of his father parts the smoke and the flames.

"I thought that you'd never show!" Tyler shouts his expression now a little more at ease.

"Yeah well there's enough good men heading to the water plant kid,"

"Plus Scapatechi is on the roof and this is personal Son!" Mason replies whilst looking out across at the burning horizon, breaking his Dad's concentration Tyler pipes up with feeling,

"Dad it's the guys, they're trapped below and running out of time, plus Rachel is still upstairs, I could hear her screams Dad!" Tyler expresses with a look of terror in his eyes. Mason unresponsive to his Son's call continues to look out towards Midtown with the feeling of revenge eating through him.

"Look Dad, the hell with Scapatechi,"

"Let it go, I need you here, with me!" He pleads, causing Mason to turn his head from the fierce fire fights below.

The thirtieth floor is now filling with deadly smoke. Rachel's screams are getting ever weaker as she feels herself drifting away, suddenly finding herself back the old dockland apartments as a frightened little girl. Just before her eyes close Rachel recalls the dark figure of a firefighter emerging from the smoke…

'Am I dreaming?' she thinks before loosing consciousness.

26

On the rooftop Scapatechi climbs aboard the chopper with a feeling of satisfaction as he peers down upon the blazing streets beneath him,

"Were to Sir?" The pilot asks as he adjusts his headsets.

"First of all let's take a little tour around Midtown, we've got great seats, we may as well use them." Scapatechi chortles before reaching for his seatbelt.

"Affirmative sir," the pilot replies beginning their ascent.

Hundreds of feet below on the ground floor JJ and the team are just about to give up all hope when Kastle notices a dark figure emerging from the flames.

"What the hell is that?" Kastle screams. To their surprise this image of hope was not Tyler, but that of the Phantom firefighter who they knew all to well from distant stories and heroic tales.

"What the…" JJ gasps as he can't believe his eyes; he knew the myth of the fallen angel but never really believed the stories. After lifting the heavy debris from JJ, Mason uses his large axe to smash burning wood and heavy concrete from the now obstructed doorway thus clearing an exit. Knowing that the exit still isn't safe Mason ushers himself beneath a burning beam and with his great strength uses his shoulder to push up the heavy burning weight and hold it in place just long enough for the guys to get out.

"Ok guys, I'm not sure how long I can hold this for; so Hurry!" Mason yells magnanimously after taking the full weight on his shoulders. JJ soon gets organised and without vacillating any longer he begins guiding his team out towards safety beneath the wing of the angel.

"Go, Go, Go!" JJ commands before sucking out more clean air from his respirator. As each one passes beneath Mason's strong arm they clearly speak the words 'thank you' along with an honourable expression of freedom. Mason looks upon them with tearful eyes whilst watching the last one leave. Within seconds Mason feels the pressures from above driving him down into the ground. Knowing that the weight is becoming too strong for him he drops to his knees to ease the tension off his back causing his legs to buckle from under him. Even in this state he watches on to see his Son's fire crew run for safety through twisted metal and burning beams; it is this vision that touches him deep within causing his mind to cast upon his own team all those years ago. Finding their spirits through his son's team he experiences an overwhelming feeling of purity; as if the only weight is on his shoulders now is the ever growing weight from the heavy beams that he holds. Freeing him from the guilt he has held for so long, his heart is now pure once more.

Looking back towards Mason JJ notices the beams collapse in around him,

"No…" JJ howls as he tries relentlessly to go back for Mason though he is restricted from doing so by his team who holds him back.

"It's to late JJ; there is nothing we can do now,"

"He's gone!" Kastle shouts. The team watches on helplessly as more beams crash down where Mason stands. They look on in horror as he disappears into the carnage.

Lombardo and his team are now closing in on the city's water plant fast, though they still have to deal with Flynt's unit of psychotic goons. Fighting furiously to gain access to the plant, Lombardo's strategy is put in place.

"Just keep killing everything that moves!" Lombardo howls; it wasn't much of a strategy, but it seems good enough for him.

On the chopper Scapatechi orders the pilot to descend,

"Take her down pilot; I want to take a closer look." With a rapid descent Scapatechi's stomach starts to hurl,

"Wow pilot, not so fast… I get air sick." The pilot gives a half smile to him self then continues on though a little more suttle.

"Sorry boss," he mutters weakly. The pilot accurately guides the chopper not far above the burning streets below, jolting sharply from side to side only missing the buildings by a few feet.

"Is this close enough for you sir?" The pilot asks with a hint of sarcasm.

"Yes, not so close though!" Scapatechi replies although feeling rather dizzy he orders the pilot to keep going. To the pilot's surprise he notices a scorched dark figure standing on an open window ledge on the second or third floor of the Shymna building,

"What the hell is that?" He gasps in a confusing tone.

"It's him, kill him." Scapatechi demands before bringing out an embroidered handkerchief to wipe the sweat from his brow. The skilled pilot makes way towards the firefighter, however Mason is already thinking ahead, and at the choppers approach he makes a courageous leap from the burning building latching his axe onto the side of the chopper. A heavy thud echoes itself through out the chopper causing the pilot to turn and face Scapatechi.

"I'll try and shake him boss," the pilot yells whilst grasping the control stick with his two hands.

Mason holds on for grim death as the pilot manoeuvres the chopper in various directions trying his up most to toss the extra baggage. Scapatechi unfastening his seatbelt scurries across to the side of the chopper were he reaches for the door handle. Sliding the door open Scapatechi twists his foot around the seatbelt before placing himself half out of the chopper were he finds the unwelcome guest. Mason tries relentlessly to hold on, swinging back and fro until he manages to grip tightly unto the doors ledge and to his surprise he is met with the sinister face of Scapatechi which seems to glow red from the ferocious flames bellowing from below.

The insane mobster doesn't hesitate in taking a few shots at Mason with his Tommy gun, only missing him by inches; Mason ducks for cover.

"To hell with this..." Mason roars as he tries against all odds to make his way to the other side of the chopper, keeping himself hidden he thrusts his axe up into the under belly of the aircraft, using his axe handle to grasp he easily swings himself to the other side, out of the way of Scapatechi's barking iron he manages to grasp onto the opposite door ledge resting momentarily to catch his breath.

"I think we've lost him boss," expresses a very relieved pilot. No sooner do the words leave his mouth Mason emerges from the far door taking Scapatechi by total surprise. The two men now face to face seem quite civilised; well at least for now.

"So we finally meet," Scapatechi confidently says with a smug grin on his face as he raises his Tommy gun pointing it directly at Mason's huge worn body.

"It's the end of the line for you." Mason tells Scapatechi before forcefully kicking the gun from his hands sending it out into the red sky were it plummets to the burning streets below. Meanwhile at the controls the cunning pilot slowly reaches for his gun, seeing this Scapatechi tries to keep Mason talking for another few seconds giving the pilot time to aim at the firefighter, though Mason's instincts tell him something is up. Just before the slimy pilot has a chance to pull the trigger, Mason swings his axe around knocking the gun from his hand sending it the ground were it slides past Mason's boots stopping only a few feet from Scapatechi.

"Holy shit, I'm out of here," shrieks the cowardly pilot; opening the door and making a jump for it. He plummets about one hundred feet until he eventually lands on a giant air cushion the fire department had set up for people that were trapped in the surrounding buildings. Shocked police officers look across at the commotion to find a shaken up pilot.

"Wait a minute… I know this guy; he's with the Scapatechi crew!" An officer shouts with great pleasure.

"What are the odds of this, huh?" Another adds before slapping the cuffs on him.

Mason and Scapatechi begin to engage in heavy smash mouth fighting, though Mason does have an unfair advantage. Mason throws heavy punches into Scapatechi sending him to the deck pleading for his life,

"Please, you've won, don't kill me." Scapatechi begs. Towering over his limp body Mason stares deep into the monster before him, deep down Mason knows the lawful thing to do, however his gut was telling him different, with his axe raised high above Scapatechi he decides to do the right thing,

"Thank you thank you," stammers Scapatechi who was glad to be alive. A few seconds later and a quick jolt from the now out of control chopper throws Mason from his feet giving the cunning Scapatechi a chance to retrieve his gun from the ground. Scapatechi manages to pump off a few rounds hitting Mason in the shoulder sending him towards the deck.

"ARRRGGHHHHH…" Mason yells as the bullets lodge in his shoulder.

"Well, well, well… Now look at the big man, I should have finished you off that night in dockland when I had the chance!" Scapatechi expresses with a psychotic look in his eye.

"Give it up you maniac, the entire state will be looking for you; do you really think you are going to get away with this?" Mason roars whilst placing his hand on his wounded shoulder.

"Oh how I remember that night in dockland, it only seems like yesterday when I gunned down Francez and Mr Dice" Scapatechi reminisces as he toys with Mason with the barrel of his gun.

"I knew your face firefighter but it took me a while to place it then it finally came to me, right after I shot you down." Scapatechi begins to laugh uncontrollably.

"Where would that have been?" Mason quizzes as he turns his head from the gun.

"Oh that's the beauty of it firefighter,

"Remember that tragic bus accident all those years ago?" Mason listens on as the fiery pain in his shoulder continues eating its way though his pain threshold.

"Well I was the one that got away!" Scapatechi whispers right into Mason's ear; if looks could kill Scapatechi would be a dead man as Mason stares right through him with dagger eyes.

Climbing to his feet Mason clutches Scapatechi by the throat, undeterred by the countless bullets that Scapatechi is now pumping off, Mason manages to throw the crazed lunatic to the back of the chopper head first, as Mason slowly reaches for his trusty axe he senses the bullets burning through his body. Waiting for Scapatechi to climb to his knees, Mason with the little strength he has left swings his huge axe towards Scapatechi's neck sending his severed head from the chopper were it free falls to the streets below before landing amongst a squad of goon who look on with terror.

Dropping to his knees Mason crawls towards the pilot's seat where he notices the C.B. Flicking it onto the appropriate channel he calls out for help.

"Lombardo, are you out there?"

"Come in…" Mason holds his breath as he tries to deal with the pain.

"Come in Lombardo, god dam it!"

"How the hell do I fly this thing?" Mason demands, hoping Lombardo will hear his call.

Back on the ground Lombardo hears a familiar voice laced with static, he instantly reaches for the nearby C.B.

"Go ahead, Lombardo here!" He hastily responds

"Back out, get the guy's out of there, I think I've got a plan!" Mason shouts down the C.B. praying to God that Lombardo will hear the call.

"Mason, were the Hell are you?" Lombardo shouts hysterically into his radio.

"Look up old friend," Mason replies with calmness to his voice. As Lombardo looks up he sees Scapatechi's chopper which looks wildly out of control and is heading straight for them.

"You are one crazy son of a bitch Mason!" Lombardo mutters into himself before he instinctively gives the necessary orders to his men.

"Get your asses out of here, now!" Lombardo howls.

Flynt and the other gunmen laugh and sneer as the police and fire department start to retreat; they assume they have won their little battle but Flynt soon changes his reaction when he suddenly notices that Scapatechi's chopper is flying straight for them and out of control.

On the chopper, the now bleeding and bruised Mason tries his hardest to keep the chopper heading towards the water plant.

"Lombardo, are you out there?" Mason asks his eyes feeling heavy

"Tell me this, what's the status on Tyler and Rachel, did they make it?"

Mason asks with a wishful tone though Lombardo notices his voice becoming much weaker.

"I'm sorry big guy, I've just received word from JJ and the team that neither Tyler nor Rachel has come out of the Shymna building, we also heard that we lost a lot of guys down in Broadway both F.D. and P.D. somebody's got to do something Mason and fast." Lombardo replies in a morbid tone. With this news Mason reaches inside his fire jacket pocket and pulls from it a rugged faded picture of his daughter Lydia. Placing it on the control panel in front of him he once again looks for his daughter's strength...

***

"Daddy... I'm tired," a very drowsy Lydia murmured. Mason could barely hear her as her voice was so weak.

"Yes baby, its daddy, I am here!"

"I am here for you; try to stay with me..."

Mason was flooded with emotion and tears as he knew he couldn't let go, not yet, not like this. Behind him he noticed his crew cutting there way into the car that had collided with the bus, Mason over heard Lombardo on the C.B.

"It was a getaway car the mob had used after their bank robbery, was just a terrible tragedy that they smashed into a school bus, we've got two of them still trapped in their car, F.D's just cutting them out now, though the driver is still at large, over and out."

The blue lights of the 911 emergency vehicles seemed to light up the street causing Lydia's eyes to flicker.

"That's it baby, stay with me…" Mason pleads as he holds his baby in his arms.

By now Lydia was drifting in and out of consciousness leaving her vision blurred and her every breath fighting for air. The two held tightly when Lydia slowly raised he tiny hand pointing towards the flashing blue lights on his engine, her now cold lips whispered the unforgettable words,

"Look Daddy… Blue Angles…"

At that her lips moved no more. Mason's heart sank deep into his stomach as he watched the life leave his only daughter. On instinct he lay with her in silence, unresponsive to the paramedics he closed his eyes and held her tightly…

∗∗∗

Opening his now heavy eyes Mason pulls him self to his feet, somewhere deep down inside him he finds the will to live. Just as he grinds his heavy body towards the choppers side door he is met with sparks and horror when the choppers propeller blades cut straight through Flynt and his gang, shredding them to pieces before the chopper itself penetrates the huge water silos, causing millions of gallons of water to rush through the Midtown streets. Gushing through the streets the powerful force of the water attacks the fire like a battle of the elements causing a heavy cloud of smoke and ash to form which gallops through the streets covering everything in its path. Lombardo's squad, who are now soaking wet, quickly round up what's left of the terror gangs.

"How do you like that commissioner, huh?" Lombardo shouts as he tries to light up his wet cigar, his feeling of accomplishment soon sinks as he turns and gazes at what is left of Scapatechi's chopper.

"Jesus Mason, what the Hell did you do…?"

Throughout Midtown, scores of firefighters continue tackling what's left of the blazing buildings when a silence falls upon them as the shadow of a man walks through the now smoking streets carrying the body of a young woman; the man is none other than Tyler Hope, carrying the body of his only love, Rachel, in his arms. In the midst of all the commotion Tyler drops to his knees and lays Rachel carefully on the wet street cradling her like a baby, he holds her hand and strokes her face whilst whispering the words,

"Don't leave me baby," into her ear. It doesn't take long for other firefighters make way towards the two creating a rather large crowd

"Sir please let her go, we'll take her from here," one of the paramedics calmly asks…

27

The distant echo of a soft trumpet breaks the silence of the morning's ceremony. Tyler stands surrounded by his team looking on at the fallen heroes that lost their lives during the Midtown massacre. The old preacher once again reads words of courage, freedom and Hope. During the ceremony Tyler turns his head and kisses Rachel on the lips.

"What's that for." Rachel asks surprisingly.

"I thought I lost you Rachel…" Tyler replies in a heart warming tone. Rachel tilts her head to the side, and smiles lovingly.

"Plus, I won the bet," he whispers before kissing her once more.

"You certainly did my hero." Rachel replies whilst hooking onto his arm. Looking across the memorial garden Tyler notices Dale and Lombardo in conversation.

"Give me a few minutes will you Rach, there is something I've got to do." Tyler asks as he strokes her face.

"Yeah sure Tyler, I'll be right here waiting for you," she replies whilst biting her bottom lip. As she watches Tyler make his way towards the two men she can't help but sense something strange, though she can't quite put her finger on it. As Tyler approaches Dale and Lombardo they instantly turn to greet him,

"Your Dad sure is one tough old man Tyler!" Lombardo says with a glare of hope in his eyes.

"Here, he wanted me to give you this." Dale adds, whilst reaching into his shoulder bag. To Tyler's amazement it is a worn out old baseball and mitt.

"He never forgot you Tyler, ever… Or your Mother." Dale says while handing it over Tyler who is now laced with emotion. Looking into Dale's eyes Tyler finds the answer he is looking for.

"He made it, didn't he Dale?" Tyler whispers in a wishful tone whilst looking around frantically for his old man,

"Come on kid, no ordinary man could have survived that!" Lombardo adds, whilst throwing Tyler a wink.

"That son of a bitch, I knew it, I just knew it," Tyler replies with a burst of excitement before asking,

"Hey guys, one more thing,"

"Can you pass on a message for me?"

"Sure kid, sure." Dale and Lombardo both answer, then look at each other with a puzzled glare.

"Just tell him that Rachel doesn't need an angel no more, and thanks, thanks for everything. Tyler says with a gasp of air causing his eyes to water.

"He knows that Tyler, he can finally let go now." Dale replies whilst extending his arm in search for a hand shake. Dale and Tyler now shake on it before turning to Lombardo to do the same.

"Thanks guys, now you two take care." Tyler suggests as he backs off into the congregation to pay his final respects once more.

"What was that all about Tyler?" Rachel questions whilst hooking back onto Tyler's arm.

"Nothing Rach, I was only passing on a message," he replies whilst locking fingers with Rachel.

"Oh right, a message to whom?" She asks as she rests her head on his shoulders.

"A fallen angel," he replies, his voice now firm with an underlying quiver.

Just before the coffins are lowered Rachel feels sincerity in his voice and does not respond to his words, they both remain silent as the soft honourable music grace their ears.

On a buildings ledge high above the streets below, a dark figure kneels between two Angel-like gargoyles watching over the city from a distance. With his axe propped beside him and his long fire jacket blowing in the gentle breeze, just like the flag of his country in the wind, a firefighter stands tall and hastily makes way towards an orange glow on the horizon. May he bring hope, courage and justice to all?

THE END...

January 20th 2007, my birthday coincidently, I couldn't sleep at all that night, I remember having the feeling of another year pass just like the year before and the year before that. However this one was different! I had reached the dreaded quarter of a century, that's right I had hit twenty five. Only a baby I recall my father saying, but to me it was tragic, to me it was old, though I did celebrate in style. To enlighten you on my inspiration I will have to take you back to about nine months before my birthday, just another mind numbing shift in a mindless factory, surrounded by drones if you will, filling the machine with little silver shiny disks then unloading the same disks over and over and over again, the twelve hour shifts seemed to last for twelve days, however I did have a beautiful girl friend working near by to keep me sane and also a handful of close workmates that shared my views on the drone like community working throughout the factory like robots. These close workmates that shared my views had befriended me nearly the minute I had started, these were good guys, and they shared my humour. They were probably one of the reasons why I had lasted so long in the factory. I don't know if any of you are familiar with Ken Kesey's 'One flew over the coo coo's nest?' But if you are, I most certainly felt like R. P. McMurphy, and the factory was like a nut house. Due to the strict management who seemed to write the rules as they went along, it felt like there was no winning with them, I often referred to them as educated idiots, or in some instances, uneducated idiots, as they only climbed the corporate ladder by stepping on those below them. There I was chained to a machine loading those little disks when I heard a yell from up the floor, it was one of my close mates Ken McKay, he had brought a piece of A4 paper with him and stuffed into my back pocket on his way past, knowing I was due a break pretty soon I was patient and waited until I reached the locker room before I unfolded this page of mystery.

If you know me, you will know that I am a huge Sylvester Stallone fan, especially for his alter ego 'Rocky' I remember reading an interview with Sly that reached me, he said that his whole life he had tried to be somebody, to be recognised for being him and time after time he had failed until one evening when he was watching a Mohamed Ali boxing match all that had changed. With a virtually unknown contender who was predicted to be knocked out by Ali in a few rounds stunned everyone. This unknown had gone the distance with probably the greatest fighter that the word had ever seen. Though Stallone had found something else in this underdog, well a day and a half of writing later I believe Rocky was born. Apparently MGM had requested that Burt Reynolds would play the part, but I guess Sly just wasn't having any of it. Thank god huh. Well anyway back to the piece of A4 paper Ken had stuffed into my back pocket. The title read ' Back for one final round' I thought to my self that it was some kind of joke, Stallone making another Rocky at the golden age of 59, but the more I read the more I understood what he was doing. He was completing the famous anthology, at first I thought it was for the fans, well maybe it was, but deep down I knew it was more about him, completing the journey for his fictional character, closing the chapter on an amazing story, he was kind of completing himself in a way. A few months later the news came out that 'Rocky Balboa was to hit the big screen on January 19th, a day before my twenty fifth birth day. It was then the plans were set for an ultimate birthday celebration. Time wasn't long in passing by, I remember it well, the talk of the party kept my spirits high in the factory as did it my pals, the plan was on the 19th to meet at six o'clock in a local American style steak house called O'Brien's were ten pre booked cinema tickets would be distributed to the guys over plates of big steaks and cold beer, then after the movie we had plans to go back to my house were I had a pool table and poker table set up in my attic conversion, I remember praying that there would be no hic ups. There we were sitting around the table waiting for the steaks when we I suddenly found my self in conversation with a few of the guys. The topic of discussion was life and work. I remember one of the guys discussing how we should invent something; something great! I recall mentioning the guy that created Spiderman etc, Stan Lee, how he must be so proud of his creation and that he will always be recognised for it, that guy made it! For me the ultimate goal is to have my own creation, a creation people will relate to, maybe even give them a little hope. Across the table a few other guys had application forms in for the local fire department, I over heard them say that it would be an amazing experience, the feeling of saving a life and also getting out of the factory; however it was extremely hard to get accepted into the fire department as Northern Ireland is such a small country and so many people wants in. It was at that moment in that steak house, listening to everyone's dreams and ambitions when the character of Mason Hope was born. I started work on the creation on January 20th 2007…

I strongly believe that the concept of this fictional character 'Mason Hope' will aspire to great things. My personal desire is to complete a trilogy novel collection, three complete novels hopefully finding its way towards a strong comic audience. My ultimate dream is to see this character be brought to life by the magic of Hollywood; I have overwhelming confidence that this novel will be a huge success and indeed harvest a strong fan base. If marketed properly and envisioned in the way I see it, this project will reach the sky.

FIREFIGHTER
THE FALLEN ANGEL

Available at

www.authorhouse.com
www.theinspiragroup.com
www.amazon.com
www.heroicnovels.com

Forum

www.heroicnovels.com/forum

Lightning Source UK Ltd.
Milton Keynes UK
UKHW040644161020
371701UK00001B/53